Cat's Outta The Bag

Elle Carolyn

Cover Art and Design by charisjb.studio

CONTENTS

—❖—

DEDICATION

In loving memory of Chicken Nugget.

The best kitty anyone could ask for, even if he didn't hook me

up with my own love interest before he had the audacity to leave

me too soon.

Trigger Warnings/Content Warnings

Trigger Warnings/Content Warnings

Even though writing is a form of art, I don't believe that I can ethically create something and pretend that it might not be harmful. Trigger and content warnings are essential to ensuring I've done my part as a writer to protect my readers, because some themes and content in this book may be triggering. Below are the TWs/CWs I've identified. Please only read if you feel safe to do so:

Graphic Sexual Content (always consensual)

Swearing (no slurs or discriminatory language)

Brief descriptions of miscarriage

Brief descriptions of the struggle to get pregnant

Transphobia (implied, not on page)

Self-harm (implied, not on page)

Brief descriptions of car accidents

Brief mentions of medical procedures (not graphic)

Death (related to the emergency medicine field)

Gun violence (not on page)

Mentions of police violence against People of Color (not on page)

Fear for a loved one during reports of gun violence

Chapter 1

Alexis

Bang. Bang. Bang.

The door practically rattles off its hinges.

Ooh. Ominous. Sounds like the opening line in a murder mystery. In reality, it's just my food being delivered on time. It's my first day off in ten days, and the idea of putting effort in to cooking was just not an option. I barely made it out of my house this morning to get expensive coffee, let alone go get the groceries necessary for a proper meal.

I take stock of myself before getting up to answer the door. I have on my unicorn footy pajamas (with the feet cut off; I get too hot), my hair is in a messy bun that I couldn't be bothered to straighten up, and there is a suspicious stain on my sports bra. Am I going to answer the door like this? You bet.

After a quick check at the peephole to confirm it is indeed my delivery person, I open the door just enough to say hello and grab my food. I did not count on the fact that I ordered enough food to feed an army and would have to open my door significantly wider than usual to get it all inside.

This was a mistake.

My sweet, loving, adorable, DEVIL cat took advantage of the extra inch of space and streaked past into the hall before the delivery person, or I, realize what's happening. And before I could even shriek her name, she'd slipped through the closing elevator doors, startling the poor neighbor inside, likely on their way out, excited for a regular Friday night. I only catch a glimpse of their shocked expression before the doors close with a ding.

For a moment I stand there stunned, briefly wondering if the person I saw is my new neighbor. And then I remember, my cat is currently sharing an elevator ride with said stranger, and I'm just standing here, like an idiot.

"FUCK!"

With the speed of Katie Ledecky in an Olympic pool, I grab my food, set it on my counter, and dash out after my spawn of Satan cat. She will regret this!

There's only one elevator in this building, so I take the stairs at a breakneck speed. Luckily, I only have five floors to race down, so I make it in record time.

I startle Jerry, our night security guard, and several residents as I burst out of the stairwell, ready to strangle my fur baby. I have so much momentum, I nearly slam right into the person who shared the elevator with her. And when I look up into their eyes, my brain completely short circuits.

Holy. Fuck.

Jason MOTHER FUCKING Adams is holding my cat like a baby, stroking her furry tummy.

For a moment, I consider that this is a hallucination brought on by sleep deprivation. But no, after another moment of complete silence, Jason Adams is still there, holding my cat. His sandy blond hair is styled in that way that screams sex, but classy. His blue eyes are crinkled as he smiles down at the furry devil in his arms. He's dressed to go out, and here I am, standing in front of one of Hollywood's biggest movie stars in my goddamn unicorn footy pajamas. Target will PAY for making these things in adult sizes. I suddenly feel like I'm stuck in the rom-com he starred in a few years ago where the female lead, who's a complete disaster, somehow manages to snag the dude who has it all. I know, I know, sexist much? It definitely wasn't his best role to say the least. And why the hell am I even thinking about this right now?

"That's my cat." That's right, folks. I'm meeting one of the most attractive men in the entire world, and the first thing to pop out of my mouth after I stare for an uncomfortable amount of time is: *that's my cat*. Jesus fuck, this guy is going to think I'm crazy.

"Yes, I gathered that. A little escape artist, huh?" His voice is like smooth whiskey, not that I actually know what whiskey tastes like, but that's something people say, right? Whatever the correct descriptor is, it sounds fucking amazing and makes my insides clench. The corners of his eyes crinkle, and I have to take a moment to not swoon. Fuck, this man is maybe more beautiful in real life than on screen.

"Sometimes, I think she does things just to embarrass me. Thank you for grabbing her; hopefully, she didn't fight you in the elevator." There. That sounds normal, even if I'm still a bit breathless. I did just sprint down five flights of stairs.

"We had to have a bit of a heart-to-heart first, but once I explained we needed to work together, for your sake, she came quite easily." He smiles, like actually smiles. Oh fuck, I'm dead.

There is an awkward pause. And with a jolt, I realize that this is the appropriate moment where I grab my cat and leave. Instead, I'm staring.

"Well, uh –" My brain and mouth are just not connecting right now. This is so embarrassing. "thank you, I'm just gonna –" I reach to take my cat from his *very* muscular arms when the she-demon makes my night worse. With a cry that would impress a banshee, she twists her black body out of his arms and SIDE KICKS HIS FACE before making a beeline for the front doors.

"SLINKY, NO!"

With speed I didn't know I possessed, I chase after my cat and dive for her, sliding across the lobby floor like a seasoned MLB player sliding to home plate. Within milliseconds I grab my cat, sit up, stuff her down the front of my onesie, and zip it all the way up, effectively trapping her. It's over in a blink of an eye.

The lobby is dead silent.

Jerry is staring. Jason is staring. The delivery person, who has reached the lobby by this point, is staring. My cheeks flame with embarrassment. Oh my god, what just happened?

With as much dignity as someone who just slid across a public space to catch their cat can have, I stand up, one arm awkwardly supporting Slinky's ass to keep her from sliding down a pant leg or something equally humiliating. I bend forward slightly, my free hand making a little wave motion like I'm taking a bow after a performance.

Like I said, my brain is short-circuiting.

This is Hell.

When I straighten, I notice Jason is pulling his hand away from his cheek, looking at his fingers, which are dotted with blood. Slinky is dead. She scratched a movie star's fucking face! They have those things insured! I think.

"OhmygodIamsosorry!" I rush up to him, quickly grabbing his hand and dragging him over to Jerry's desk. "Jer, can you grab the first aid kit under your desk for me?" Neither man has spoken yet, though Jerry does quickly produce the kit. With my free hand, I pull out antiseptic wipes, Neosporin cream, and a sterile Q-tip swab.

"Fuck, again, I am so sorry. Here, turn your face to the side. May I?" I hold up the wipes and wait for him to turn his face before I start cleaning the wound. "Sorry, this is going to sting." Jason lets a little huff as the wipe comes into contact with the raw skin, but lets me do my work otherwise. It's not as bad as I initially thought, just one long scratch across his right cheek, and it's already stopped bleeding.

One-handed, I open the swab and add the Neosporin cream. When I look back at Jason, he's staring at me with the oddest expression. Almost as if he is in awe of me. Which is silly.

As I gently smooth the cream onto the cut, I say, "Make sure to wash this properly when you get home tonight. Occasionally, cat scratches can cause cat scratch fever if you don't wash them properly. It's caused by the *Bartonella henselae* bacteria and generally clears on its own, but you'll want to keep an eye on things for the next few days. If you get a fever or the skin swells at all, go to your doctor. But honestly, I've been scratched countless times and always been fine." I give him my reassuring doctor smile and end up locking eyes with him.

I can't tell you how long we stood there, dumbly staring at each other, but Jerry's not-so-subtle cough tells me it was way longer than what is socially acceptable.

"Again, I am so sorry about my dumb cat. If you end up needing a doctor, please have your bill sent to me; I'm happy to pay it."

"That won't be necessary. Getting scratched is expected when handling cats." He shrugs as if this whole scene wasn't the most bizarre ten minutes of his life. "Well, I have to go; thanks for patching me up. Bye, Slinky." He gives Slinky a chin scratch, whose head has popped out of the collar of my onesie, and exits the building, whistling as casual as can be.

What?

Jerry and I exchange a look. A moment later, we are in stitches; we're laughing so hard I might pee myself.

I'm wiping tears out of my eyes, barely catching my breath. "Please do me a solid and delete the security cam footage. That was so bad." Our lovely security guard, Jerry, is bent over in his chair wheezing. "Sorry, love, no chance. But I will be replaying it over and over again whenever I get bored. That was something else."

I roll my eyes, chat a bit longer with Jer, and then head back to my apartment. My food is most definitely cold by now.

It's not until I reach my door that I realize that in my haste to catch my hateful cat, I've forgotten my keys. This is just not my night.

With my head held high, I head back downstairs and have to ask Jerry to let me back into my apartment. It takes at least two minutes for Jerry to stop laughing and get off his bum to help. I can't blame the guy, though; if I had just witnessed that scene, I'd probably piss myself from laughing too.

What a night.

CHAPTER 2

JASON

What a night.

And I don't mean the absolute insanity that was my neighbor chasing after her cat and generally being the most chaotic person I have ever met.

Nope.

My night consisted of me showing up to three separate parties, looking for my fucking agent, who insisted we talk tonight about possible upcoming projects. I'm nearing the end of filming for my current movie and need to pick out my next few projects. The asshole is one of the top agents in L.A., but that means he can be tough to pin down. Since my recent, VERY public breakup last month, I've been avoiding the party scene, so I was not thrilled when I had to party hop after him, just for him to be too drunk to even have a coherent conversation.

Fuck, I hate this part of Hollywood life.

"Hey, Jerry," I call out to the security guard who witnessed the crazy earlier tonight, but keep my focus on the elevator. I'm not in the mood to rehash anything and just want my bed.

"Wait, Mr. Adams!"

Fuck me. I close my eyes briefly and remind myself that this guy has no idea how horrible my night was and doesn't deserve my bad attitude.

"Yeah, what's up?" I ask, turning back to his desk, where he's waving something at me. It's a piece of paper, I think?

"Ms. Masters left this for you. She asked me to give it to you since she didn't know your apartment number, and I'm not at liberty to give it out." I smile, knowing he's talking about the woman who was the only bright spot in my day. I can still picture the look of absolute concentration on her freckled face as she took care of the scratch. Fuck, she was adorable.

"Thanks, Jerry; I appreciate it." I snag the white envelope with my name written in neat penmanship on the front, then head back straight for the elevator.

I don't open the envelope until I'm safely home, and I can't help but smile at the note inside the generic card.

Dear Jason,

I wanted to write a quick note and express my deepest apologies... again. Slinky is the devil sometimes, and tonight you were her chosen victim. Thank you for being such a good sport about it earlier, but I want to reiterate that if you end up needing medical attention, please send any related bills to me (I'm in apartment 505). I hope the rest of your night was enjoyable and not filled with a homicidal psycho jungle cat hellbent on destruction.

Yours Sincerely,

Dr. Alexis Masters

P.S. I have absolutely no idea why I just wrote my name like that. I was not trying to flex, I swear. It was automatic, and written in pen, so not erasable... this post-script is awkward, why am I still writing?

P.P.S. I want to also add, since this note is already embarrassing, that while I know who you are, I will not be broadcasting that Jason Adams is living in my building. Everyone deserves privacy... hopefully this didn't make things even more awkward... I'm going to stop writing now.

I can't help but laugh. This was exactly what I needed.

Lately, it's felt like things are falling apart. First, with the breakup between Vanessa and I. And now with my inability to pick my next project. I'm in danger of stalling out, which could kill my career. I shouldn't be letting my focus drift, but I'm not sure I could stop myself if I tried.

Alexis is the epitome of adorkable, and her cat is the perfect kind of feline crazy. I honestly had no idea what to do when Slinky first entered the elevator with me. When I looked to see where she came from, all I saw was Alexis' horrified look. Then the doors shut, and Slinky was asking to be picked up. It was one of those times when a pet knew something we didn't because when I say that I have never been so attracted to someone in my life, I am not exaggerating.

Something in Alexis called to my soul, which is why I was basically speechless the entire time.

So now the question is, how do I get to know her without making her feel like I'm taking pity on her after the admittedly embarrassing cat-gate episode?

I'm in my bed staring at my ceiling when a light bulb goes off. I quickly text my sister for her help and fall asleep smiling.

It takes a couple of days to find what I am looking for, but I can barely contain my excitement when I do. The store clerk nicely packages the item up for me while I write a note for Alexis. When I'm back in our building, I set the gift outside her door, knock, and sprint back to my apartment. I just know that if I'm standing there when she finds the present, she'll get self-conscious.

Now I wait.

God, I hope she uses the phone number I gave her.

I can't remember the last time I was this nervous about a woman.

The wait is going to kill me.

Chapter 3

Alexis

It's been a long day.

Hell, it's been a long week. This is my fourth and final year of residency in emergency medicine, and I can honestly say this week was the worst in my career. After Slinky's attempt to ruin my life, within the first two hours of my next shift, there was a ten-car pile-up, with my E.R. being the closest level-one trauma center. We lost four patients that day, performed two limb amputations, and gave thousands of stitches. I've seen death plenty of times, both traumatic and peaceful, but this was on another level. I ended up needing an emergency session with my therapist just to cope.

And it just got worse from there. I spent two nights in the on-call rooms rather than sleep at home, we were so busy. It got to the point where half the staff was convinced we'd been cursed or that a planet was in retrograde, making our lives a living hell.

The reality is this is what emergency medicine is; some days or weeks are just shit.

But what matters is how many people we heal because that far outweighs those we lose.

I'm still wrapped in my thoughts of work when I step out of the elevator and stop dead in my tracks. There is a box outside my door.

With a bow.

What the hell?

If Dateline and true crime podcasts have taught me anything, it's that you can't trust random packages you weren't expecting.

I slowly inch my way to the box, probably a bit irrationally afraid that the vibrations of my feet will set off the bomb that is most definitely inside. Once I'm actually at my door, I can see there is a note tucked under the ribbon.

As slowly as humanly possible, in case it's attached to a trip wire, I slip out the card. I'm only a little embarrassed that I squeaked in fear once it was free. I have a moment of panic that the card could be filled with anthrax, but then I remind myself that it wouldn't be attached to a box if that were the case. I think.

Taking a deep breath, possibly my last, I open the envelope and take out the card.

Is this in Latin?

I'm not exactly sure how long I stand there deciphering possibly the worst handwriting I've ever seen (and as a doctor, that's saying a lot). But once I read it all, I can't help but smile like an idiot standing in my hallway at ten in the morning, completely alone.

The box isn't a bomb, so that's good. But even better, Jason Adams doesn't think I'm a complete psycho.

Dear Dr. Alexis Masters,

I think anyone who has the title of a doctor should use it. You earned it. Never be ashamed to flex your accomplishments.

Even though I was pretty quiet the other day, I thought you and Slinky were really cool, and I hope to run into you more often. In the box is something I thought you both would like; my sister has one and her two cats are obsessed. I hope you like it.

Your Friend,

Jason

P.S. I'm in apartment 511, in case you ever need something. And I'd love to see a picture of you and Slink enjoying the gift sometime, 310-555-9595.

I have to shake myself to get moving and actually open my door; I'm so giddy over this note. I set the box on my counter and greet Slinky, who comes running when she hears me. Even though she has an auto-feeder that can last for a couple of weeks, she definitely misses our cuddles when I'm gone at work. She chirps and weaves between my legs, giving me an affectionate rub.

"Now, Slinky, we've got a gift to open. I'm still salty at you about taking off and scratching Jason's face, but since he clearly doesn't hate us, I might be prepared to forgive you."

She continues to rub against my legs as if to say *yeah, duh, Alexis, you never stay mad at me.* And she's right. Can't hold a grudge to save my life.

"Alright then, let's open this gift." I rip into the wrapping (I'm always too excited to be mature about it), and I'm speech-less when I finally get to what's inside the box.

Tears in my eyes.

You can chalk it up to the emotional stress of the last few days, but this is so thoughtful I can barely hold it together.

I pull out the gray sweatshirt to show Slinky. "Look, sweet girl, this has a kitty pocket so you can walk around with me!"

I immediately shove my body into the sweatshirt and open the zipper pocket. Then, before she can run away, I snatch up my cat and stuff her in the pouch, zipping the opening almost shut but with enough room for her head to pop out. Which it does. I snap a quick selfie, and hands down, it is the cutest picture I've ever taken with Slinky. Shockingly, she seems happy in the lil kangaroo pouch.

Trying not to overthink it, I shoot off the selfie and a quick text to Jason so he knows I got the gift, then get to work on tidying up the apartment.

I definitely don't send six follow-up texts in less than one minute.... Nope, definitely not.

CHAPTER 4

JASON

I'm in my trailer reviewing the stunt choreography for my scene later today when my phone pings with a new message. When I notice it's an unknown number, my pulse picks up. Every cell in my body is hoping it's Alexis.

I can't help but laugh when I open the text and see the image. Alexis has the sweatshirt on, and Slinky's head is just peeking out of the pocket. Her smile is enchanting. I pump my fist in celebration, irrationally happy that she likes it, like a complete douche. Don't come at me.

I don't even read the text itself. I'm so busy being mesmerized by her smile. But once I do, I can't help but laugh again. This woman.

Alexis: Hi Jason! Or Jason's phone person. Thank you so much for the gift, Slinky, and I are in love!

Alexis: Celebs have people manage their phones, right?

Alexis: Fuck, maybe that's just social media?

Alexis: Fuck. Now I'm embarrassed.

Alexis: Also, to be clear, Slinky and I love the sweatshirt. Not you. We are not, and I repeat, are not, in love with you.

Alexis: I need to stop texting now.

Alexis: [sweating awkwardly emoji]

I'm laughing for a good minute at her rapid-fire texts before being able to follow up.

Jason: Glad to hear you and Slinky love it so much! And no, I don't have people who manage my phone for me. I do, however, have a social media team.

Jason: Got any more behind the scenes of movie stardom questions for me?

There, that sounds sufficiently encouraging without being condescending. At least, I hope so.

Before she can text back, there's a knock at my door, signaling they're ready for me on set. I shoot off one last text, so she knows I'm not ghosting her and head out.

When we wrap for the day, I am off like a shot, heading back to my trailer as quickly as possible. Some actors bring their phones to set for downtimes between takes and whatnot, but I've made it a habit to leave it in my trailer. When I'm acting, I want to be as focused on the scene as possible.

I am relieved beyond what is rational to see two texts from Alexis. What the hell is happening to me?

Alexis: Have a good day on set!

Alexis: And you have no idea what can of worms you just opened… be prepared for a lot of questions. [winky face]

She gave me the perfect opening I need. I shoot off one last text before heading home.

CHAPTER 5

ALEXIS

I blink. And blink again.

Is—

Did—

Did Jason Adams, Hollywood actor, winner of two Oscars and one Golden Globe, ask me out? To lunch?

I pinch myself just to make sure I'm not dreaming. Because let me tell you, the number of intensely steamy dreams I've had about him over the last few days borders on unhealthy.

Nope.

I am not dreaming. Holy cow.

I need to be cool, cool as a cucumber. Being friends with a movie star requires a bit more sophistication than I am currently capable of, but I'm committed to playing the part.

"Be cool, be cool, be cool, be cool."

I write and rewrite a reply six times, SIX TIMES. But once it seems sufficiently cool, calm, and collected, I send it off.

It takes Jason nearly an hour to text back, and my anxiety over what I sent him is through the roof by the time my phone chimes. It's across the room, shoved between the couch cushions because I was obsessing over it so much. Honestly, if someone had recorded the swan dive I took over the arm of the couch to go grab my phone, you'd be impressed.

Jason: Sounds great. I'll get us a reservation and text you the details. I'll be wearing a ball cap and sunglasses to fend off the rabid fans, just in case you can't find me. [winky face]

It's embarrassing, but I audibly squeal over his reply. We're just getting lunch, but he's taking the time to plan it and make sure we at least can spend some of the time in peace before people realize he is there. We've treated a few celebrities at the hospital over the years, and I've never sympathized with them more than when they're just trying to seek medical treatment, and the paparazzi and fans are swarming.

Celebs may have signed up for public life, but that doesn't mean they should be constantly mobbed, especially when seeking medical care.

Before I can shoot a text back, there is a knock at my door.

I look at Slinky, who's lazily watching me from her window perch as if she would know who it was. I'm not expecting guests; in fact, I need to leave in the next thirty minutes for my shift at the E.R.

"Alexis? You home? It's Jason."

Fuck, even through the door, his voice sounds amazing. My whole body shivers. Before he can decide I'm not home, I rush to the door and yank it open, surprising him so much he gives a little jump. I can't stop the laugh that escapes at the thought that I scared Jason Adams.

"Hi."

"Hey."

We both smile like idiots at each other.

A neighbor down the hall exits their unit, jolting us out of our respective reveries.

"So," Jason rubs the back of his neck, "I was parking in the garage when I replied to your text and then just thought I'd drop by and say hi since I would pass your door." He pauses and notes my scrubs, "oh, are you just getting back or on your way out?"

"I have to leave in about twenty minutes for my shift. But I'm glad you stopped by. Want to say 'hi' to Slinky?"

I step back, silently berating myself; why the hell would he want to greet my psycho cat? Without hesitation, he crosses into my unit and heads straight toward Slinky. In the blink of an eye, he is luvin' her up, giving chin scratches and murmuring sweet nothings into her ear.

And fuck if I'm not a little jealous of my cat right now.

Oh man, that's messed up.

"Well, I'll get out of your hair. I'll see you at lunch tomorrow. Bye, Slinky." He gives her one last scratch before heading for the door.

"Bye, Jason, I'll see you tomorrow." I smile and wave as I shut the door, absolutely not taking a moment to watch his nice ass as he walks away, definitely not.

An hour later, I am wrapping up my charting for a kid's broken arm and referral to the pediatric wing for treatment when my watch chimes. His text scrolls through on the tiny screen.

> **Jason:** We'll be eating at Maison LaCroix at 12:30. I hope you like French cuisine.

I smile like a lunatic for the rest of my shift.

I'm going on a lunch date with Jason Adams. I can't wait.

CHAPTER 6

JASON

I am incredibly nervous.

In fact, I don't even remember being this nervous when I first started acting.

I changed my outfit five times, for fuck's sake.

I'm already seated when she enters, and I can't help but drink her in as she shyly waves, following the host to our table. She looks radiant, dressed in a plum sundress, white wedge sandals, and her shoulder-length dark brown hair loosely curled. Her green eyes absolutely pop.

Like a gentleman, I stand and pull out her chair, inhaling her intoxicating scent as she brushes past me to sit. I have to resist leaning down and burying my face in her hair. We aren't *quite* there yet.

"Hi."

"Hey."

We both smile as if soaking each other in. Or at least, I know I am.

"Have you been here before? What's good?" She breaks eye contact to look down at her menu, chewing her bottom lip. I almost groan; why is that so sexy?

"Um," I clear my throat, concentrating on the menu, "Pretty much everything I've had here is good. If you haven't ever tried *escargot*, theirs is delicious. The chef is from the Alps, so there are some good hearty meals, too."

"I'm game to try new things. Should we maybe share the snails and then both order something else?"

"Sure, that sounds great. Do you want any wine or something else to drink?"

"Normally, I'd say yes, but I start a week of overnight shifts tonight, and it always goes better if I concentrate on hydrating."

We both take a couple of minutes to peruse the menu, then place our orders with the server when they join us. While she's ordering, I take a moment to admire her. She's always so kind. I've heard her say thank you at least ten times since she arrived, and her smile it's never fake. She doesn't rush through her order but patiently watches as the server writes things down, only saying the next part once she's sure the server is ready. Not many people I know would be that patient, and I'm positive it makes her a good doctor.

Once our server departs, I ask, "So, if you have a string of overnight shifts coming up, why aren't you sleeping right now?"

"Oh, well, I'm usually too keyed up about the overnights in the first place to really sleep during the day. And I kind of need that first overnight to get my body to sleep during the day. I let myself lay in bed all morning until I needed to get ready for lunch, so I try to take it easy. I hydrate and make sure I eat good meals. Even if I did sleep, the first couple of overnights are always an adjustment." She abruptly stops, as if she's suddenly self-conscious.

"Don't stop now; I've never been friends with a doctor, let alone an Emergency Medicine Specialist. Tell me more." I give her an encouraging smile and feel a thrill when she takes a deep breath, seemingly ready to give me all the details. I love hearing her talk.

"I could talk your ear off about E.R. Medicine, so stop me at any point."

An hour later, we're both in hysterics. "The poor kid had locked his jaw wide open. And not even for anything remotely salacious!" she blushes, realizing she just brought up sex. After a beat, she pushes on, and I can't help but smile. "This kid and his buddies were competing to see who could open their mouths the widest. *Not* for anything sexual; they were insistent. They wanted to prove how much food they could fit in their mouths. But because they were teenage boys, they figured opening their mouths as wide as possible and using a ruler to measure was the most logical way to do it."

She shakes her head, dabbing at the corners of her eyes. "And of course, this one ended up with lockjaw, which made them all panic. They were beside themselves by the time they came into the E.R., thinking his jaw was permanently stuck open and he'd have to get all his nourishment from a feeding tube. Honestly, I think I spent more time calming them down than I did actually treating the lockjaw. The best part?"

Her eyes twinkle, and I know whatever she says next will be good. "Once we had unlocked his jaw and gotten him comfortable. His friends played *We Are the Champions* on a phone and presented him with a makeshift trophy made up of blown-up gloves, tongue depressors, and other random supplies they'd charmed out of the floor nurses. THEN he accepted the trophy and even gave a little speech. By the end, everyone in the E.R. that day was clapping and cheering." We're laughing so loudly that we're getting dirty stares from fellow diners. But I honestly couldn't care less. We are having a blast.

We're silent for a beat, finishing up our meals. She ended up loving the *escargots* as much as I do, which normally would be great, except we fought over who got to eat the last few. She won.

"I've been talking this whole time, and the point of this lunch was for me to ask questions about the behind-the-scenes life of a movie star."

I shrug, making a gesture that says go ahead. "I'm an open book Alexis, shoot."

She taps a perfect finger against her perfect chin, mock thinking of her first question. I guarantee you she has a whole list on her phone. Don't ask me how I already know this about her, I just do.

"Ok, I got one. Why did you start acting?"

A wave of unease washes over me. How the hell did she manage to ask the *one* question I hate answering?

"Really? This is something you can Google to find out. Both my parents are actors. It's a family legacy. My sister's an actress too, but she's in the Indie scene." I tip my head from side to side, trying to ease the tension suddenly in my shoulders.

"Sure, that might be the public answer, but I want to know *your* answer. When did you first realize you wanted to follow in their footsteps? Did you do theater in school or just jump straight to the big screen?"

I sit back, contemplating what to say. I've never admitted to someone how I actually feel. It twists me up inside sometimes.

"Honestly? It wasn't ever really a choice. My parents always referred to us as an acting family. And as soon as my sister and I displayed promise, they were bringing us to auditions. My first job was actually on a T.V. show. It was canceled after the first season, but I showed enough talent that I landed my first movie role the next summer. Then my sister played a secondary character is this obscure indie film that I think ten people have watched, and the rest is history, I guess." I shrug, hoping she'll move on.

She chews her lip again, studying my face closely. "Hm, ok, I'll let you have that answer. But someday, I *will* get the real one out of you." How the hell she can already pick up on my half-truths is beyond me. I might be in trouble.

She moves on to much easier questions, and we settle back into comfortable conversation. At one point, the dessert menu comes around, and we both order *Tarte Tatin*. She made it very clear that we were not sharing this time.

As we finally head out of the restaurant together, my hand naturally ends up at the small of her back, as if I'd done that a million times before. I open the door for us and lead her out.

I hand the valet my ticket, then reach out to do the same for Alexis. She looks at me with confusion. "Your valet ticket? You drove, right?"

She blushes, "Oh, um, no. I mean, yes! But, I parked up the street. I, uh, I've never had my car valet parked before." She presses her lips tightly together like she is trying to keep from saying anything else.

"No problem, Doc, I'll walk you to your car." I turn to the valet at the station, "I'll be right back. Just want to make sure she gets safely to her car." They nod and turn to help the next guests.

"Jason," why does my name on her lips make me hard? "You don't need to walk me to my car. It's literally right there; you can see it."

I shake my head, place my hand back on the small of her back again, and start walking to the little Honda Fit she pointed to. She rolls her eyes but keeps walking.

We get to her driver's side door and turn to face each other. I am consumed by the need to kiss her, even though we aren't there yet.

"Thank you for lunch. I had a lot of fun." She smiles up at me, and I can't help but smile back. "I'll be craving *escargot* for the rest of the week now." She giggles as if that was the craziest thing.

A gust of wind picks up and blows some of her hair into her face. Without thinking, I tuck it back behind her ear, then let my hand run down her arm. Before either of us can say anything else, I see something out of the corner of my eye that catches my attention. Without turning too much, I get a better view and see that it's a paparazzi rapidly taking pictures of us. My blood is suddenly *boiling*.

"Don't freak out, but we've got a pap taking our picture." She freezes, and I drop my hand. Fuck. I was hoping we'd have more time to get to know each other before the public forced their way in. "I'm going to call my P.R. team and get them working on a statement. Are you able to check your phone at all while working? I want you to give the statement your stamp of approval before it goes out. Shit. I'm so sorry, Alexis. This is the worst part of my life. Are your social media accounts private? We – "

She reaches out and gently grabs my bicep, giving it a quick squeeze. "Slow down there, Jason. Take a breath. I walked into this lunch knowing that this was a possibility. I accepted that. It's not your fault some dude is across the street, taking our pictures to sell to gossip magazines. I'm not super active on social, but all my profiles have been private since I created them. It's going to be ok." She gives me another squeeze before unlocking her car and opening the door. Before she sits down, she turns back to me. "I'll keep the volume up on my watch and will look for a text from you. I'll try my best to step away and give it a once over, but I trust you." She smiles and adds, "It's going to be ok. I had a wonderful time at lunch."

She finally gets in, and I step away as she starts her car. My phone is already out, and calling my people as she pulls away. And while I'm still pissed, she eased the worst of my worries.

"Petra? It's Jason. We've got a situation here."

Chapter 7

Alexis

"Shit."

HOLLYWOOD'S MOST SECRETIVE CELEB PARADES MYSTERY WOMAN AROUND TOWN WHO IS SHE?

Intermixed with the completely dramatized portrayal of our lunch are the shots of Jason and me at my car. The angle of the shots makes us look way closer than we were and definitely gives us a romantic leaning. Even the one where Jason is scowling directly at the camera with my hand on his arm. We look like a couple; it doesn't matter that we've barely known each other two weeks.

Sources close to the new couple say they've been keeping things under wraps.

I snort at that line; sources close to the couple? What the fuck? These are straight-up lies. I should ask Jason how he handles these kinds of articles.

In a statement made this morning, Jason stated he had lunch yesterday with a close friend and that any claims of a relationship were unfounded. He kindly asks that the media back off and focus on his upcoming feature film Agent Smith: Total Takedown, *in theaters March 16. But we know our readers, and this reporter is determined to give you the juicy deets. Stay tuned for more about Jason Adams' mystery woman.*

What the actual fuck?

"Decaf latté for Sarah?" The barista sets my drink down and turns back to the next drink. I'm not exactly sure what possessed me to give a fake name at this coffee shop, but now that I am looking up from my phone and seeing a couple of stares, I'm glad I did. Never hurts to throw people off the scent, I guess.

I put my head down and hustle back home, hoping no one's following me. Fuck, this is messed up.

Four fucking hours later, and I am still too keyed up to sleep. Slinky is keeping me company, sensing something is wrong, but even though I'm exhausted, my body won't relax.

Despite myself, I pull out my phone and text Jason. Maybe he can help,

> **Alexis:** Hey, are you home? Or are you on set today?

I don't have to wait long before he replies.

Jason: Not on set today. They're filming scenes that don't include me. Is everything ok?

Part of me doesn't want to unload on him; I'm sure he's stressed about this too. But the fact is, he's had the media covering his life for decades now, and I'm a newbie. He'll have a better handle on this than I do.

Alexis: I saw the 'Reporter' article and am just feeling off about it? I'm trying to sleep but can't relax. Any advice?

His response is almost immediate.

Jason: You got a Blu-ray or DVD player at all?

Random. But I'll bite.

Alexis: Yes? Not sure if the Blu-ray player still works, but I have it hooked up. Why?

He doesn't reply, and five minutes later, I'm resisting following up. He isn't my boyfriend, and honestly? It would be a stretch to even call us friends. I have no right to expect quick responses from him, or any at all.

Just when I think he's completely abandoned me, I hear a knock at my door.

"Alexis? It's Jason. I've got something that might help."

I can't help the huge smile on my face when I open the door and find Jason on the other side holding what looks like a movie, a box of microwave popcorn, and a few different types of candy. He smiles right back.

"Whenever I'm feeling overwhelmed with the media, I watch a comfort movie that I don't really have to watch to know what's happening, and it helps turn my brain off. I brought *Princess Bride*, which is not only a classic, but one of my favorites."

I smile and blush. This is so sweet. "Sounds perfect." He grins back.

"Here, take the movie and start getting us set up on your couch. I'll pop the popcorn."

We spend the next few minutes in companionable silence. Part of me wants to be shocked at how easy and comfortable this is, but the rest of me knows this just feels right. As soon as the popcorn is ready to go, Jason joins me in the living room, and we settle in.

The opening scene is just finishing. Buttercup is asking Wesley to get her that jug when Jason's arm comes down around my shoulders.

"Is this ok?"

"Yeah." *More than ok.* I snuggle in deeper, pulling the blanket around me tighter. His light cologne surrounds me, oddly comforting. Quickly, I start to relax. I feel so safe that I don't even notice that I'm falling asleep.

Hours later, my alarm goes off, jolting me awake. It takes me a minute to figure out where I am.

I'm in bed, fully clothed, and despite being slightly disoriented, I actually feel well-rested. On the pillow next to me is a note written in Jason's nearly indecipherable chicken scratch.

Alexis,

You fell asleep pretty quickly and would not wake up. I hope it's ok that I picked you up and put you in your bed. I know you're still on overnights and need to sleep. I didn't want to leave your door unlocked though, so I stole your keys (sorry, it felt creepy, but I also couldn't handle the thought of someone being able to come in while you slept). I've left them at the security desk with Marcus, who confirmed he would make sure they went directly into Jerry's hands once he is on shift. I hope you feel better after sleeping. We should talk about how to move forward soon. Again, I'm so sorry for dragging you into the public eye.

Have a good "day" at work.

Jason

P.S. I oddly feel like I can't write you a note without a post-script. HA!

I smile at the P.S., realizing we now have a "thing" that we do just for the two of us. We aren't even officially friends! I feel like a teenager. I'm so giddy over this.

I find myself humming as I go about my "morning" routine. I give Slinky some snuggles, then head out my door, using my spare key to lock up. I keep it hidden in a junk drawer, so there's no way Jason would have known where to find it. Some days, *I* can't even find it.

Jerry has a sly look on his face when he hands me my keys, but he doesn't say anything beyond the usual pleasantries we exchange, which is a relief.

Despite my raw emotions over that article, I feel much lighter as I head to work.

Chapter 8

Jason

How are there no 24-hour florists? This is L.A., we might not officially be the city that never sleeps, but we sure act like it.

I'm not exactly sure what possessed me to think that I should send Alexis flowers during her night shift, but now I'm frustrated. It doesn't help that my earlier phone call with Petra felt incredibly unproductive. Basically, her advice was, "Just lie low for a while, Jason. Soon someone else's drama will pull their attention away. You know the drill."

Honestly, this whole situation is just asinine. I'm starting to suspect that I like this remarkable woman but that my celebrity status might scare her off before we get the chance to even see what we could be. And because of that, I'm feeling even more trapped by my life.

I'm not exactly sure when this feeling started. When I was in high school and first realized how little choice I had in my future, I felt apprehensive but hopeful. My parents clearly loved their jobs as actors; they got to fly all over the world for films and festivals. We had the financial security that most families dream about. So what if I didn't exactly enjoy it? I would grow to love it, be successful like my parents, and it would be fine. But every year, I felt worse, and the last five especially have felt almost unbearable.

What I couldn't admit to Alexis the other day was that I hated acting. And if I'm being honest with myself, if I couldn't act again for the rest of my life, I'd be fine. Happy even.

As if she could sense my thoughts, my mother's ringtone blares through the apartment. What the hell is she doing calling me at one in the morning? I hesitate a beat before sighing and answering; something could be wrong.

"Mom, is everything alright?"

"Hello, dear. And no, nothing's wrong. Why would you ask that?"

"Well, it's pretty late here. You usually don't call me at one a.m."

"Oh no! I completely forgot about the time difference. I'm so sorry darling, your father and I are in London for a premier, and I wanted to talk to you. Do you want me to call back later?"

And this is why it was so hard to say no to them when they pushed us into acting. My parents genuinely love us and want us to be happy. Sure, they pressured us into acting, but it was because, to them, that was what we did. We were an acting family. And the thought of disappointing them made me feel sick.

"It's ok, Mom, I was awake anyway. Glad everything is fine. What did you want to talk about?"

"Well, a couple of things." She pauses, and I immediately know at least one thing she wants to talk about. Fuck me.

"Honey, you know your dad, and I try not to read any gossip mags. They're nearly all telling lies, and we obviously know to ignore them. But.... Well, this article is about you and a mystery woman. I guess I'm having a hard time understanding what's real and what isn't. You two seem pretty cozy in these photos, and I would just be so happy if you were actually dating her. Are you?" Her voice is so hopeful that I almost lie. She has always been my biggest champion when it comes to love and always encouraged me to be open and honest about my feelings in relationships. Seeing me happy with someone would make her day.

But I can't lie. Because even if I want to try something with Alexis, that's a discussion we need to have privately before anyone else has a chance to stick their nose in.

"I hate to disappoint you, Mom, but she is just a friend." If I leave it at that, she might decide the leave things alone.

Knowing my mom, she'll pretend to leave it alone, then ambush me in a few days with questions. And when that happens, she won't stop until she has the answers.

I can hear her brain running through possible scenarios from here. She's exhausting.

"I'll accept that answer for now because I know you'll tell me know when you're ready. But just so you know, I think she's adorable."

I roll my eyes, she can't just leave it alone.

"Good to know, Mom. Thanks for letting me have just a bit of privacy. So, what was the other thing you wanted to talk about?"

Another pause, the phone muffles for a moment, and I can just make out my mom calling for my dad to come into the room. Great. This means it's serious.

"Ok, I put you on speakerphone so your father can hear. Honey, I ran into Steven last night, and he told us you haven't signed on for any new projects. That at the moment, you don't have anything booked. What's going on? Are you alright?"

I stifle a sigh as best as I can. Of *course,* my parents would run in to my agent on a random night in London. And, *of course,* he'd decide to open his mouth. He's probably hoping my parents will pressure me into picking a project. Fuck this.

"Nothing's wrong. I'm just not feeling the projects he's brought me recently. Not the right vibe."

My father jumps in. "What's the real reason, son? Money not good enough? Do you need me to talk to some of my buddies and see what roles they have coming down the pipe?"

Shit, they're not going to drop this. Either I admit I don't want to act anymore, or I need to pick a project soon.

"Sure, Dad, go ahead and put out feelers. Not exactly sure what I am looking for, I just know what Steven's gotten me lately just aren't for me."

I can't see them, but I know both my parents are nodding in agreement. Once they both reached stardom, they quickly learned to only take on roles that suited them. Acting is not easy, and you should really want a role if you want to do well. And when you reach the level of my parents, and I guess me, you get to be picky.

I pretend to give a huge yawn, loud enough that they'll hear me and let me off the hook.

"Sweetheart, you sound tired. I'm sorry we called you so late your time. We'll hang up, but don't forget when we get home, I want to chat more about this girl you're seeing."

I almost laugh, she will never let this go, I guess.

"No worries, but I need some sleep. Love you guys, enjoy London."

"Bye, sweetheart. I love you."

"Goodnight, son."

They hang up, and it takes all of my self-control to not throw my phone against my wall. I don't know what to do with my career.

But what I *do* know is that Alexis and I have a lot to talk about.

CHAPTER 9

ALEXIS

> **Jason:** Hey, hope your day is going better. I don't know what your schedule is like this week but hoping you'll let me take you out for coffee or lunch again?

> **Jason:** I totally understand if you don't want to be seen out in public with me again. No pressure.

I've stared at his texts for way too long now, but I can't seem to make myself reply. My heart is screaming to take a chance. My brain... well, it's screaming, *PUMP THE FUCK-ING BRAKES!* I'm feeling more than a little confused.

In college and med school, I was so focused on doing well and landing my dream residency, I barely thought about dating. And the one time I tried... well, it didn't go well. And now, with Jason being such a public figure, there's a part of me, a rather large and loud part of me, that worries that it will eventually destroy whatever we try to build. And that there's a very real possibility it could destroy the career I've worked so hard to build.

And yet... the thought of never seeing him again. Of not knowing where this might go fills me with dread. I don't want to wake up one day and regret that I let fear get in the way of something good.

Before I can stop myself, I shoot off a quick text back and then toss my phone to the other end of the couch, earning a glare from Slinky as she naps on my lap. I guess I moved too much for her.

> **Alexis:** I'd love to get coffee. There's a cute local place a few blocks away that we could go to if you're free tomorrow morning (my shift starts later in the day).

Within moments, my phone dings. Wow, that was fast. But when I dislodge the supremely unhappy Slinky to read his message, it's not Jason, it's Dr. Beauford, the other resident in my program.

> **Beauford:** Hey, I know this is super last minute, but is there any way you can cover my shift tomorrow? It wouldn't add more than a few hours to your week and would get me out of a tight spot with the wife. I really appreciate it.

A week ago, hell, even a few days ago, I would have jumped at the opportunity to cover his shift. I've never been one to pass on an opportunity to be at the hospital. My dad's frequent advice echoes through my brain '*Textbooks and classes are great, but the only way to truly learn to be a great doctor is to practice in the real world, with real stakes.*' Sage advice from one of the best doctors I've ever known, and I don't just think that because he's my dad. He's a legend at my hospital, even after nearly five years of retirement, you can still hear people referring to something he said or did on a nearly weekly basis.

Doubt swirls in my gut as I stare at Beauford's text. Maybe I can cancel quick with Jason before he can reply. He'd understand. But as I'm about to backtrack, his reply comes in.

Jason: Great! I can stop by your apartment around 9:30? Or, meet you there. Whichever you're more comfortable with.

I can't help but smile at his text. He clearly doesn't want to seem too eager, but it shines through anyway. My heart begins to race, and I feel a little jittery. I reread Beauford's message and get a little ticked off. I've covered for him more times than I can count, and for the first time, I'm annoyed he asked. The man always seems to ask last minute. And now that I'm rereading it, I notice how he takes it for granted that I'll say yes. *I really appreciate it*. Like it didn't even cross his mind that I'd say no.

Before I can stop myself, I decline Beauford, and tell Jason he can come pick me up at my apartment door. It takes hours before I feel less sick about letting my career take the back seat for once.

***

At nine thirty sharp, I hear a knock at my door. I feel butterflies as I take one last look in my entryway mirror and fluff my hair. I blow a kiss to Slinky, who definitely ignores me, and peek through the peephole just to confirm it's him. I only feel a little gross for taking a hot second to watch him as he rocks back on his heels, hands shoved in his jean pockets. He looks excited, but nervous. Which is good because that's exactly what I feel. Who knew? The stars... they're just like us!

I yank open the door and quickly step out, shutting then locking it in record time. I don't trust Slinky anymore, even when she's asleep in her cat tree.

"Sorry, I just don't feel like repeating how we met today." I smile, hoping I don't come off as rude for not inviting him inside. Or greeting him. Shit, I'm bad at this.

"Completely understandable." He chuckles, running a hand quickly through his hair. "If she was my cat, I'd probably do the same thing."

And just like that, my nerves dissipate. He gets it. I have to remind myself he's not just some Hollywood fuckboy, out of touch with reality. He's down to earth, kind, and, well, normal. I don't have to put on a show for him, and from what I've gathered, if I tried, he would walk away.

So, when he takes my hand in the elevator, and asks if it's ok, I say yes, even though my palms are a little sweaty from nerves. Nerves that die down a little more when I notice his palm is a little sweaty too.

As if he can read my thoughts, he looks down at me and we both share a sheepish smile. Like we know, the other knows, we're nervous and that's ok. And by the time we make it to the coffee shop, our palms are dry and our smiles are just smiles.

***

"Wait, wait, wait!" I throw my hands up, laughing so hard my stomach hurts. "You just blurted that line out, hands down the funniest line in that whole movie, and they kept it in the final cut?"

Jason shrugs, grinning into his coffee cup. "It happens more often than you think. Some of the best lines and scenes are spontaneous. And more often than not accidents."

"Ok, so then what's your favorite thing you've done on set that was a total accident but made it to the big screen?"

He sits back and looks out the window, clearly contemplating his answer. Then his eyes light up as he finds the memory he's looking for. Just as he opens his mouth, a couple of kids edge up to our table, clutching their phones nervously.

"Are—" one the kids' voices cracks, as he stares at Jason in awe. "Are you Jason Adams?"

Jason smiles, "I am. You kids looking to take a photo with me?" They all nod quickly, completely tongue tied. Jason glances at me, eyebrows raised, clearly asking for permission. I smile and hold out my hand to the main kid, so I can use their phone to take the picture. The interaction lasts maybe five minutes, but the group leaves looking like they just won the lottery.

"Sorry about that. I know not everyone loves it when fans interrupt." He takes a sip of his coffee and reaches over to entangle our hands across the small table. "When it's kids, I try to always take a moment to take a selfie, or sign something. Even if I'm in the middle of something. I hope that's ok." He can't quite meet my eyes, like he's embarrassed or nervous that I'll react badly.

"Jason, the only time I'll ever be annoyed by you taking the time to do something with fans is if *you* don't want to do it. Otherwise, never feel bad about it. At least not with me." He slowly nods, clearly digesting what I've said. While he does, I observe the café around us. And for the first time since we arrived, I notice all the people glancing our way, clearly discussing us. Maybe they've been watching us the whole time, or maybe they only took notice once those kids came over. Either way, I'm suddenly a little on edge, not sure what to do.

"Try to ignore them." Jason's quiet voice pulls me back to the table. To us. His hand gently squeezes mine. "For the most part, people will leave you alone if you make it clear you're not 'open for business' so to speak. Kids, don't always pick up on those cues, but that's ok, I'd much rather take pictures with young people, than adults." He smiles reassuringly, and I find myself smiling back. Because of course the wonderful human in front of me makes sure to always take time out of his day for young fans.

"That reminds me of a question I've been curious about."

"Shoot."

"How come you live in an apartment building with a bunch of strangers? And I always thought celebrities had bodyguards following them around to keep away the crazy women in unicorn footie pajamas." I smirk as he laughs. We both know I looked completely nuts that night, even if it seems to be turning out ok.

"It's all personal preference, really. My parents keep security staff around most of the time, unless they're at their home on Catalina Island. I don't know if you remember this in the news, but when I was about ten, my mom had a stalker. They eventually caught the guy, and she's fine, but because of that, having security makes them feel safe. Isla hardly ever feels the need since she's in the Indie scene and often flies under the radar, unless we're all together as a family." He takes a sip of his coffee before continuing.

"Mostly, I do without. During premiers, especially for franchises like *Agent Smith*, I'll hire on some security. Fans tend to get a little more intense then. And honestly, I often relied on Vanessa's security team when we were together. But for the most part, I hate the idea of being followed around. It just feels wrong, and invasive. As for living in an apartment building, it's not ideal. But after Vanessa and I imploded, I needed a place on short notice, and this was the best we could come up with. And I have to say, it's worked out pretty well." He nudges me with his foot and smiles, making me melt.

Before I can reply, my phone alarms dings. "Shit, has it been that long already?"

"Time to go?" I nod, and he gets up without argument, grabbing our dishes and bussing them to the counter. I'm shocked we've been here for as long as we have, I didn't even notice. Usually when I have a weird start time for a shift, I'm anxiously watching the clock until it's time to leave. I feel a little twinge as we leave, hand in hand, wondering if he can distract me this much now, what happens when we really start dating?

What am I getting myself into?

***

The next day, I'm passing Dr. Beauford and an attending in the hall when I overhear their conversation.

"I'm not exaggerating when I say I'm in the doghouse, man. Why the hell does it even matter that I missed a three-year-old's dance recital? She won't remember it anyway. And I tried to get my shift covered..."

Their conversation trails off as I get farther away, a sick feeling settling in my gut. I already felt guilty when I got on my shift yesterday when I heard it had been a crazy morning. But now learning that I caused Beauford to miss his kid's dance recital?

What the hell am I doing? Am I really risking ten plus years of study over a guy? It's not until I'm home with Slinky that I'm able to be a bit more rational. It's not my fault Beauford didn't plan better to get his shift covered. I'd bet my favorite stethoscope he knew about that recital well in advance, and did nothing about it until his wife put pressure on him. The guy is a good doctor, but he's an ass most of the time. I don't get what his wife sees in him.

By the time I'm starting to drift off, I've mostly set aside my guilt. But there's still a tiny voice in the back of my mind, screaming that I'm about to lose it all.

CHAPTER 10

JASON

Normally, I make it a rule to never read tabloids, especially when they're about me. But it isn't just about me anymore, so I force myself to look at the garish headline again.

SPOTTED GETTING COZY

HOLLYWOOD STAR IS CAUGHT ON CAMERA

WITH THAT MYSTERIOUS WOMAN AGAIN

WHO IS SHE?

I groan, again. Why can't they just leave us alone? Clearly someone, or maybe even more than one person, took pictures of us at the café yesterday. I don't bother reading the article, I'm sure it will just piss me off more than I already am.

I consider texting her, but if she hasn't seen this already, I don't really want to tell her about it. Considering her reaction to the "Reporter" article about our first date, I'd rather she be blissfully ignorant about this one. I know she'll be home soon. Maybe I'll check-in once she's home and we can watch a movie together and discuss it.

Across the room, my phone rings, blaring "You're a mean one, Mr. Grinch", and I instantly smile. When Isla was a teen, she went through a major "I hate holidays" phase, and we all called her a Grinch that year. She hated it then, hates it now, but I can't seem to bring myself to change her ringtone. What else are brothers good for, if not to torture their little sisters whenever possible?

"Hey, Isla," while I keep the ringtone, I know better than to actually call her a Grinch, I like my balls where they are.

"Hey, doofus," her voice crackles a bit, like she has bad service. Which, now that I think about it, I'm pretty sure she's out in the wilderness camping with her boyfriend. What the hell is she doing calling me while she's away from the city?

"I'm calling because I saw that new article about you and that gorgeous babe. Wanted to check in."

Ah, that explains it. Although I'm surprised she spends any time on the internet when she's out there.

"Thanks, Isla, I'm ok. Honestly, I'm more worried about Alexis."

"Oooooh, she has a name! Partick!" I hear her smack her boyfriend in the background, "did you hear that? Her name is Alexis!" I have to hold the phone away from my ear to save my eardrums. Her little sister screech never fails to hurt.

"Yes, Isla, believe it or not, she has a name." Despite the shrieking, I'm excited that she called. I love my sister, and we're pretty close, so getting to finally tell her about Alexis is fun.

"Gah! I'm so happy for you! I know it's not official, or anything, otherwise you would have told me, but do you like her?"

"Yeah, I do. I really do. She's so smart. And funny, and kind, and she has a cat who is the devil incarnate and somehow also the sweetest thing you'll ever meet. I think... I don't know, but I think we could be something." I leave it there, not sure what to say next. Alexis and I still need to talk seriously about what we want out of our fledgling relationship. Hell, she might not even want to date me, considering all the media shit she's going to have to deal with.

"She sounds amazing! What's her last name? I want to stalk her socials." The phone suddenly muffles, like someone grabbed it. In the background, I can just make out Patrick saying, "Babe, you can't just go stalk her socials. Just wait until you meet her. Don't be creepy." I laugh. Patrick is the calm to my sister's storm. He keeps her grounded in a way she's never had before.

Growing up, we had a hard time with our parents' near constant travel. I dealt with it by basically inhaling books, doubling down on school, and trying my best to emulate them. Isla, in classic baby of the family fashion, acted out whenever possible. She evened out as she became an adult and started working on more projects, but it wasn't really until she met her patent attorney boyfriend that she really started to settle. Two years ago, she wouldn't have been caught dead sleeping in a tent somewhere in the mountains with no access to running water. Now they spend every chance they get out in the wilderness.

"Hey guys?" I wait until I hear that they've put me on speaker phone and are listening instead of bickering. "How did you handle Patrick being shoved into the spotlight?"

"Hmmm, Partick can chime in with his own thoughts, but for me, it was most important to make sure he knew I was here for him. That I was willing to go to bat for him with the media, no matter what. Do you remember early on, when they tried to dig up his family history and make it look like I was somehow too good for him? And then I went on my TikTok account and made sure they all knew that I supported him, period. And that I was willing to sue anyone who tried to say even one bad thing about him?" I nod, even though I know she can't see me.

"I'm going to assume you just nodded. But anyway, I did that not just to show people they would need to go through me to get to my man, but it was also to show Patrick that I wasn't ashamed of his family, or him. That I... I love him more than anything and would do anything to make sure he's safe and happy." There's a hitch in her voice as she finishes her story. That was a dark time for them. They almost didn't make it through, but now they're well on their way to being the most nauseatingly in love couple I've ever met.

"Honestly, I was more worried about how my family's past might hurt Isla than how it affected me. But knowing that your sister didn't care what anyone thought, and she just wanted me for me, helped a lot with handling the media. Now, of course, they mostly ignore me, since being a patent attorney is pretty much the most boring thing people can think of. Things will even out. You just need to make sure you're checking in with Alexis, and giving her whatever support she needs." Patrick is probably one of the most logical people I've ever met, and his steady, confident voice soothes some of my worry.

"Thanks, Pat. And you too, Isla. I feel better. I just hope I can be what she needs." We chat a little longer about their plans for the next leg of their hike and when they'll be back in L.A. After we say our goodbyes, I hang up, feeling a lot lighter.

Chapter 11

Alexis

"D r. Masters, can you sign these discharge papers for me, please?"

I accept the tablet from one of the floor nurses and dot my i's and cross my t's. This patient managed the sprain their ankle on a swing. They were trying to get enough momentum to go all the way around like they did as children, but didn't consider how much bigger they were and, therefore, how much muscle strength was needed for the trick. They literally strained the muscles in their calf, ankle, and foot so much that it caused the same injury as twisting your ankle while walking. Needless to say, they will not be trying that again.

I have two hours left for my last night shift, and I am so ready to be done. Thankfully it's been a relatively quiet few days, so I'm not as mentally cooked as I usually am.

I approach the nurse's station and smile when I see who just started their shifts. These women are not only amazing nurses, but they are some of my best friends too. Not every doctor gets along with nurses, and I've certainly had a clash or two with the older ones who think they know more than me simply because of their age and experience. And honestly, sometimes they do. But these ladies, they are simply the best.

Nique is my age and honestly the best phlebotomist I've ever had the pleasure of working with. Plus, she makes fantastic paella that would beat anything you could find in a restaurant. She was the first person who actually tried to be friends with me when I was matched here for residency.

Allison is one of those nurses who soothes you the second you're in her presence. She's a bit older and has three kids, which is possibly why I prefer her when I'm working with pediatric patients. She just always knows what to say to both the parents and the kids to put them at ease. Something I'm still learning, to be honest.

Last is Tristan, who rounds out our group of four. Younger than me and Nique, she excels at ortho cases. Truthfully, she should specialize and be on the orthopedic floor, but she always says that she enjoys the E.R. more. She was assigned male at birth and struggled, landing herself in the E.R. more than once. She feels like so much may have been different for her back then if she had a nurse like her in the E.R., someone who could see the pain and understand it, not dismiss or ridicule it. She might have been able to get better help and start living her truth sooner.

All three are absolute rockstars, and I am so fortunate to know them.

"Hello, ladies! Did you see the baked goodies I brought in at the start of my shift? I tried to bring enough so the day nurses would get some too." I'm looking down at my tablet, scanning the intake information for my next patient, so I don't immediately notice that my friends are staring.

It's the complete silence in response to my greeting that clues me in.

I look up and find three pairs of eyes looking at me with a mixture of curiosity and frustration.

"What?"

All three blink at me as if I should know why they are giving me these looks. *What the hell is happening?*

Nique is the first to crack.

"Don't you dare 'what' us, Alexis Sophia Masters. You damn well know what!" She opens her eyes even wider as if that's supposed to make it clearer.

"Nique, seriously, I don't know. I'm on my last overnight shift out of six, and I am running on fumes. Why are the three of you looking at me like that?"

They all gasp, as if I'm the dumbest person they've ever met. I'm usually not this dense. I think.

"Alexis, my love, my light, you've broken the best friend code." Allison grabs my hand and weirdly pets the back of it as if trying to console me.

"Seriously, what are you talking about?"

All three look at each other, then turn back to me. And it's in the split second before they open their mouths that I realize what they are talking about. This should be fun.

"When were you going to tell us you *know* Jason FUCKING Adams?" All three women manage to say it at the exact same time as if they were creepy triplets in a horror film. Honestly, they must have practiced; that was too perfect. So creepy.

I sigh. I should have known this would be coming. In fact, I probably should have said something in our group chat and gotten ahead of it all. Speaking of, why the hell haven't *they* said anything in the group chat? Those articles have been out for days!

"There's nothing really to tell, honestly. We met a couple of weeks ago. It's a long story, but now we're kind of friends? It's not a big deal, seriously."

There's half a beat of silence before all three pounce.

"What do you *mean* there's nothing to tell? It's motherfucking Jason Adams!"

"Not a big deal? You have got to be kidding me!"

"You're in a tabloid article, for pity's sake, this is the *definition* of a big deal!"

They talk over each other so fast; it takes half a second for my brain to process what any of them even said. We're getting stares from fellow clinicians and patients. I really don't have time for this.

"Ok, ok, sheesh, don't jump down my throat. I need to go see my last patient of my day and head home, you three," I point accusingly, with what I hope is a stern doctor face, "need to start working. We can meet at my place tonight after your shifts and have an emergency girl's night. I promise to tell you everything then."

They all nod enthusiastically, then scatter to go do their jobs. Nique stops me before I head over to bed six, where my patient is waiting. "Alexis, when I say we want all the details, I mean we want all the nitty gritty, and I hope *dirty* details tonight. *Capisce?*"

"Prepare to be disappointed, but I won't leave anything important out. I promise."

The rest of my shift passes with no surprises, and I want nothing more than to get home and throw on comfy clothes and snuggle with Slinky. The girls will be over after eight to torture me with their questions, so I can't go complete slob mode when I get home.

On my way home, I stop at my local grocery store and have what might be the creepiest experience of my life. I'm in the pasta aisle, minding my own business when I hear something.

Or maybe I see it out of the corner of my eye first, and my brain inserts the sound of a camera shutter. Either way, when I turn fully, I am met with the sight of two people taking my picture.

I open my mouth, not exactly sure what I'm going to say or do, but the second they see that I've noticed them, they bolt. Ten seconds later, the door to the store dings as they book it at light speed out of here. They knew exactly what they were doing. Then it occurs to me, what if they followed me in? Or try to follow me home? Goosebumps break out all over my body, and I feel a little ill. Is this what Jason feels like every time someone takes his picture?

My mind is racing as I check out and head home. I check my mirrors at least fifty times during the short drive, making sure I'm not being followed. I don't even know what I'd do if I was.

By the time I reach my apartment, I feel like I'm going crazy. Without thinking, I call Jason while I scoop up Slinky and hold her close.

I get his voicemail, and leave an admittedly unhinged message, then spend the next hour snuggling my cat to death on my couch while trying to calm down. I *knew* this was a possibility when I met Jason. But I guess I naively thought that it would take longer to happen. We *barely* even know each other! Jason has only ever dated high profile women, most recently his long-time costar Vanessa Chase. I thought my "regular-ness" would protect me longer than it did, that the tabloids would ignore me because they would just assume we weren't dating. I mean come on, why would *the* Jason Adams date a regular-ole ER doctor? We're not even dating officially!

And it's not just the possibly public attention that has me worried. It's the fact that, at the moment, he is the only person I want to talk to. I'm seeking comfort from a man who might not even want to give it. And that is terrifying.

This is a Mess, capital M, and everything.

Hours later, I've showered and managed to relax a little. Laying on my floor with Slinky on my chest purring helped a lot. When my friends knock obnoxiously at my door, I feel like I can handle anything they throw at me.

So, when I open the door and see their big smiles, arms full of wine and food, I am not prepared for my response to be bursting into tears.

"Oh, sweety, we're here now."

That only makes me cry harder.

CHAPTER 12

JASON

"Fuck!" I lay on my horn as a red model T cuts me off. The driver sticks his hand out the window and flicks me off. Which makes my blood boil even hotter. I want to ram his car.

Today of all days, I just *had* to film on location, clear across L.A. from my apartment building. Not only that, but I am now stuck on the 101, trying desperately to get past this minor fender bender that has the entire freeway backed up for five miles.

Normally, I'd be at least a little frustrated; who isn't when driving in L.A.? But today, after Alexis's completely distressed voicemail, I am panicked. I *need* to get home and see her. She sounded so scared.

My blood pressure is through the roof when I finally pull into the underground parking garage of our building. I barely have the presence of mind to even lock my car before I'm jog-walking to the elevator. My focus is already on the fifth floor.

After what feels like an eternity in the elevator, I'm finally at her door. I have to force myself to take a second and breathe. She's already vulnerable, I can't go in there all fired up. It takes at least five, ok ten breaths, to finally cool down enough to feel presentable.

I can hear voices on the other side of the door, but I can't tell if it's from people or the T.V. I get my answer, though, when I knock, and the apartment goes dead silent.

A moment later, the door swings open, and I am greeted by three stunned-looking women.

"Hello, ladies. Is, uh, Alexis in there?" They just blink at me. If I wasn't so worried about my girl—my girl? I shake that thought away quickly. Now is not the time. If I wasn't so worried about Alexis, I'd laugh. Clearly, these three are a bit starstruck.

"Hi, Jason, I'm in here. If the three women, formerly known as my best friends, would let you in, you could see me." Her voice is a bit raspy, and as the three still-silent women shuffle out of the way, I see why. Her eyes are a little puffy, and her cheeks are chapped. She's been crying.

At the sight of her, I feel like I've been stabbed in my gut.

I want nothing more than to scoop her up off the couch, cradle her to my chest, and soothe her. But I don't have that right. Not yet.

So instead, I turn to the still silent women after stepping into the unit.

"Hello, ladies. It's nice to meet you. I'm Jason." I stick my hand out to the one closest to me. This seems to snap them out of their stupor, and we get through quick introductions. Once that's over, Nique, Tristan, and Allison shake off their shock and are now quizzing me full force.

Have I ever met the Hemsworth brothers? Yes.

What's my opinion on rumors that Zendaya doesn't know how to knit? Did I *see* that Smart Water commercial? No opinion, and yes, pretty sure everyone's seen it.

Did I feel like the *Agent Smith* franchise really deserved another film after killing off its only strong female lead in the last one?

They were shocked again when I told them I didn't. I had pushed to end the franchise, but because my contract included the current movie, I couldn't back out.

"So, we've got ourselves a feminist here, hunh?" Nique gives me the up-and-down as if she can't quite decide if I'm just blowing smoke.

"If by feminist, you mean I believe the absolute bare minimum would be for a multi-million-dollar franchise to not tokenize its female characters, then yeah. Although I feel like I have a few other beliefs that would be better suited to the 'feminist' label."

At this point, we're seated in the living room. At first, I sat down a respectable distance from Alexis, not exactly sure what she would want. But she quickly slid over and tucked herself under my arm, her head on my shoulder. She seems content to just sit there and listen to her friends barrage me with questions, and I can't say I mind either. This feels right.

Maybe half an hour later, Tristan does me a solid.

"It's getting kind of late; we should leave." She gives her two friends a pointed look and jerks her head toward the door.

Nique and Allison spring into action, all three practically shouting their goodbyes, sprinting toward the door. They're gone before I can even say anything back.

The second the door clicks shut, Alexis starts to shake. For a split second, I am alarmed until I hear the giggles. She's laughing.

"Are you seriously laughing right now?" I tip her chin up, so she's looking at me. I can't help but smile at the obvious delight on her face. This is a vast improvement to earlier.

"I'm sorry, I can't help it. You looked like a deer in headlights the whole time." She dissolves again into giggles, burying her face into my chest.

"Glad I could cheer you up while simultaneously feeling like I'm being interrogated by the CIA." I give her shoulders a little squeeze and hold her close. A moment later, she stills, as if realizing that she's practically in my lap, and the mood is shifting.

She sits up and scoots away, bringing her legs up onto the couch, tucking her chin against her knees, and wrapping her arms around her legs. Her expression is somber again, and I shift too so that I'm facing her directly, resisting the urge to reach out and pull her back.

"Do you want to talk about what happened today? Or would you rather watch a movie? Or sleep? I can make you some tea."

She shakes her head. Then blows out the breath she must have been holding.

"I don't even know why I'm so upset." She looks away, color leeching from her face. I hate this.

"What we're not going to do is discount your feelings. Alexis, you had your privacy violated. It's perfectly normal to be upset. Whether or not you're a celebrity, you deserve to have a private life." I want to hold her so badly, but she seems so remote now, like a tiny island in the middle of the Pacific.

"Logically, I know that. But my brain keeps trying to convince me they weren't even taking a picture of me, that I'm making it all up. I have a tendency to do that, set aside my own emotions, and look for a more logical response. I rationalize everything." She wipes a few tears that escaped the corners of her eyes, and I wish so badly that I could hunt down whoever took those pictures and make them pay. But that isn't helpful right now. Alexis needs me.

"You are not being illogical or irrational right now. We had *one* friendly lunch, and now within the span of a few days, you have strangers recognizing you and taking your picture. I've spent my whole life in the spotlight, even before I started my acting career, and I'm *still* uncomfortable when people take pictures of me without my consent. Because that's what's missing, the consent. People like to believe that people with fame sign up for this; to some extent, we do. If fans see me out and about and they come up asking for an autograph or selfie, I'm glad to do it. But it's because they've asked first, I have the opportunity to say 'no' if needed. And regardless of if it's paparazzi or random strangers, anyone taking photos of you without your knowledge or consent are invading your privacy. And that is not ok."

I blow out a breath, a little worked up and trying to keep my own emotions in check. Maybe I should just leave; Alexis doesn't deserve any of this.

"Hey, woah, where did your brain go there?" Alexis' cool, dry hand is suddenly holding mine tightly. "What were you just thinking about? I don't like that expression." Damn, she caught that fast.

"I just feel terrible." My frustration with this situation is mounting, and I can't see a solution. "You don't deserve to feel like this, and it's all because of me." *And I should keep my distance.* I don't say that out loud, letting it remain implied. Because I really *don't* want to stay away, but at the same time, I hate that being near me puts her under the microscope.

I can't look at her, I'm so ashamed of my life. I almost startle when I feel her hands hold my face and turn me to look at her. I don't see agreement or rejection, all I see is such sincere empathy I get choked up. How did I find her?

"Look, I won't lie. This has kind of freaked me out. But it's *not* your fault. That people live their lives boundaryless is their problem, not ours. And whatever we've started here, I don't want to end it before we even know what it is. *We* deserve a chance to figure that out together, and we can't do that if you pull away now. Ok?"

I'm nodding almost frantically by the end of her mini-speech and, without thinking, pull her into my lap, tucking her into my chest. She's straddling me now, but there's nothing sexual about our embrace. We're simply holding each other, seeking and giving comfort.

The mood between us shifts at some point, probably only minutes later. My hands drift from her shoulders, down her back, sweeping out, then back up her sides. I can feel her breath pick up, feathering across my skin. Her nose grazes the spot where my neck meets my shoulder, and it sends a jolt through my entire body. Hell, I didn't even know that was a sensitive spot for me. My lips come to her temple, gently peppering kisses down her cheek. She pulls back and tips her head up just enough that on my next pass, our lips connect.

Sparks, magic, whatever you want to call it, don't do this feeling justice. Her lips are pliant and soft, her bottom lip a little chapped from her chewing on it for probably her whole life. But

I don't mind because that bottom lip is now between my teeth, and I never want to let it go. But a moment later, her mouth is open, and I can't stop from exploring her. How does she feel so good?

Her hands are in my hair, nails scraping my scalp. And I groan in response. That feels amazing. My own hands have found their way to her hair and ass, pulling her so tight against me that I feel every breath she takes, every shift of her hips against mine.

Before I quite know what I am doing, I deepen our kiss, shifting us down onto the couch, both of us grinding leisurely. Fuck, we have all our clothes on, and I feel like I could come already.

At that thought, I realize now is not the time. I need to stop.

I pull back, just enough to break the seal we've created with our bodies but not disentangle completely. Her lips are puffy from our kiss, and the pupils of her green eyes are blown. I nearly go back in.

"We should stop. You need sleep; we're both emotional right now, and I don't want to mess anything up by going too fast."

"I hate that you're right." She pouts, and that almost breaks my resolve.

"You're off tomorrow, right?" She nods, thank fuck. "Great, be ready to go at ten tomorrow morning. I'll plan a day for us, somewhere outside the city and away from prying eyes. Sound good?"

She nods, then pulls me back for another kiss. It's less intense but no less enjoyable.

It's Slinky who breaks us apart finally by jumping up on the couch and letting out a blood-curdling yowl. "That's her, 'I want snuggles right now' scream." We both laugh, and I give the cat a chin scratch before getting up off the couch. I reach down and help Alexis up. Once we're both standing, I kiss her brow, then head toward the door.

"Have a good night. I'll see you tomorrow. Lock the door behind me."

She huffs a quiet laugh, practically shoving me out of her apartment. "Please don't turn into one of those dudes who thinks he's an alpha. I *do* know basic safety habits."

I grin, happy to see her mood has improved. "Nah, just a man makin' sure his lady-friend knows he cares."

We smile stupidly at each other, unable to break eye contact while she shuts the door. Once I hear the deadbolt turn, I'm able to walk down the hall to my unit. Time to plan a date.

CHAPTER 13

ALEXIS

Considering everything, I really thought I was going to struggle to sleep, especially after the heavy make-out session with Jason. But instead of it leaving me keyed up, I fell asleep almost the instant my head hit the pillow.

However, I jolted awake right before my alarm in the midst of a wet dream in which Jason and I were in the shower together. And instead of being able to roll over and finish that dream with *him*, I had to pull out my trusty vibrator to get the job done.

I won't let him get away next time.

I take a quick shower and do my simple makeup routine. Then stare at my closet for thirty minutes, wondering what the hell I should wear.

"What do you think, Slinky? Sexy or casual?" She's curled up on my bed, napping as per usual. But at the sound of her name, her head pops up and chirps. "You are absolutely right; I can go for a little of both."

I take out my plum lacy bralette and thong set, then a pair of jean cutoffs that show off my ass, and a flowy deep green tank that gives occasional peeks at the bralette underneath. Tomorrow is my hair wash day, so I throw my dark locks in a high pony. Twisting back and forth in front of my full-length mirror, I smile. Sexy yet casual—nailed it.

I'm stuffing my feet into my Converse that have seen better days when I hear his knock. A glance at the clock tells me it's ten o'clock sharp.

When I open my door, I'm caught off guard by how attractive he is. His sandy blond hair has that perfect tousled look, his blue eyes are sparkling, and his makings of a beard are to die for. I can almost feel the scrape of his stubble against my thighs. *Oh boy, Alexis, don't go there just yet.* I can see why he's often called the "Honorary Chris." If he stood next to them, he'd fit right in.

"Hi."

"Hey."

He holds up two bags and a carrier full of coffee.

"I brought us breakfast, some disguises, and coffee. I wasn't sure how you liked your coffee, so I got you three options." He smiles, stepping inside, and I'm hit by a whiff of his cologne. If I wasn't aroused before, I am now. I'm so distracted by my desire to drop everything and drag him to the bedroom; I almost don't hear him list off my coffee options. "I have here a latté, a caramel macchiato, and a mocha. Shit, I'm realizing I didn't specify the type of milk; you're not lactose intolerant or vegan, are you?"

I laugh, shaking my head. "Nope, and even if I were, I love dairy too much to give it up. I'll take the latté first, and then I'll probably drink the macchiato after. Coffee and me? We're soulmates." I'm taking the cup he offers me when it hits me. "Wait, did you say disguises?"

He wiggles his eyebrows, grinning mischievously as he hands me one bag. I peek inside and burst into giggles. This man.

Barely keeping it together, I pull out a hot pink wig and the ugliest fedora on planet earth. There are also two pairs of sunglasses that are almost comically big. When I look back at him, he has the biggest shit-eating grin I've ever seen.

"Let's have breakfast out on your balcony, and I'll give you my rundown for the day."

We get situated on my small patio set, various pastries strewn about and our coffees. Slinky is sitting at the sliding door, yowling in protest. But after the stunt she pulled last year while out here with me, she has been banned.

"Ok, so I found this county fair that is going on this weekend. It's about three hours away, but has tons of food and rides, and is in the middle of nowhere. I thought it would be fun to wear these disguises, just in case, and go have a day where no one knows us."

I can't help but laugh. He looks so confident that his plan will work. "So, what, I wear a pink wig, and you put on a fedora, then BAM, people won't see us?"

"Oh, they'll see us, but they'll be so distracted by your hair and my obvious fashion *faux pas* that they won't even look at our faces. I mean, everyone and their mother knows I wouldn't wear a fedora if my life depended on it. And the hot pink will be just bright enough to keep people from even seeing your face." He pauses for dramatic effect. "It's foolproof." He shrugs and shoves a giant bite of ham and cheese croissant in his mouth as if there were no further arguments to be had. I vaguely remember a Twitter, I mean X, battle exploding over Jason's offhand comment about his dislike of fedoras.

This is the silliest plan, but I'm so excited to see if it works. "Alright, I'm game. I'll just need a few extra minutes to braid my hair back, so this wig fits." He gives me a smug smile, and we finish our meals in companionable silence. Well, near silence. Slinky keeps yowling every few minutes, and LA is never that quiet.

Three and half hours, and a pit stop when my bladder can't handle all the coffee I've chugged later, we are at the fair. And it's enormous.

Once we get through the gates, Jason takes my hand and guides me to where all the rides have been set up. "So I'm thinking, we ride a few of these bad boys first, then once we're sick of being thrown around at Mach 5 in rickety structures, we can eat until we get belly aches."

"Sounds perfect, Hollywood." He looks down at me in surprise; aside from the one time he called me 'Doc,' we haven't really done the nickname thing. After a split second, he gives me the biggest smile I've ever seen on him. "You got it, Doc." I smile back. My heart feels so light.

***

We've ridden each ride twice before we decide we can't risk bodily harm again. We both have careers to continue. We're both laughing our asses off as we clamber out of the last coaster; at the final drop, Jason let out the loudest yelp I've ever heard. It was only surprising because he'd barely yelled on any of the rides; he'd spent most of them just grinning. As we approached the end, he leaned over and whispered, "I think I just peed a little on that last drop." I burst into giggles, which then caused *him* to start laughing and begging me to stop laughing because he was pretty sure he would pee himself. Luckily for him, we just made it to some restrooms in time.

I'll never forget the day I almost witnessed one of the most sought-after Hollywood stars pee himself at a county fair.

Wearing a fedora.

I'm still off and on giggling when he comes out. "Listen here, Miss Giggles. You would not still be laughing if our roles were reversed here." He tips up my chin and busses me quickly on the lips before gently pinching my side.

"Hey, it's Dr. Giggles to you, sir, and considering I made us stop on the way here, I doubt I'll ever be in your shoes."

"You're right, Dr. Giggles; you are simply too mature to get caught with a full bladder. My mistake." He pulls me close and begins steering us toward the food. "Anything in particular you want to eat?"

"Hmmm, something fried."

"That's like 90 percent of the food here. Care to narrow it down?"

I tip my head back to look at him, smiling sweetly, "Nope." I squeal in delight when he suddenly scoops me up, throwing me over his shoulder, and spins me around. My wig and sunglasses fly off, but I don't care in the least because Jason is now tickling me mercilessly. "Jason!" I gasp between fits of laughter. "Jason, put me down! I'll pick a food, I'll pick! Have mercy." We're getting a few stares, but not the kind that means somebody recognizes either of us. Just people watching a deranged couple goof off in public.

He finally sets me down, a triumphant smile on his face. "Great to hear, Doc. What are we eating?"

I glance around and spot the closest food stand. "I want an elephant ear." He stoops down and scoops up my fallen items, then grabs my hand with his free one and joins the line. While we're waiting, he can't stop giving quick kisses. By the time we reach the order window, my lips feel puffy, and the lady taking our order is giving us one of those knowing smiles, like she's watched our PDA and thought it was the most adorable thing she's ever seen. And honestly, I can't say I hate it.

***

Hours later, our bellies are overfull, and the sun is just setting as we get into the ancient Ferris Wheel, because we haven't risked our lives enough yet. We're silent at first, but Jason breaks the silence as we get above the crowd.

"I had a lot of fun today."

"Me too." I tilt my head up and kiss him quick on his jaw. He responds by pulling me closer and resting his head against the top of mine.

"I really like you, Alexis," he pauses, sucking in a huge breath as if getting up the courage to keep going. I find myself holding my breath in anticipation.

"I would totally understand if you say no, but like I said, I like you a lot, and I feel like we could really build something good between us. If you feel the same, I'd really like to date you.

Officially. Like labeled and everything." He winces a bit like that didn't come out quite how he wanted. He also can't look me in the eye, which I find endearing. He's so nervous. It's sweet.

"Jason, look at me." I wait patiently for him to finally turn and look down at me. One of my hands cradles his face, stroking his cheek gently. "I would *love* to officially date you."

"Yeah?"

"Yeah."

He smiles brightly, mutters something that sounds like *fuck yes*, and dives in for a proper kiss. We keep it PG as we continue our ride, but my body responds fully. It feels like it's on fire, and I desperately want our centers to meet and find relief. We're abruptly interrupted when our ride ends, and the teenage operator has to cough loudly to get our attention.

"I think that's our signal to head home."

"I couldn't agree more."

***

I must have fallen asleep during the drive back because the next thing I know, Jason is gently shaking my shoulder. "Alexis, babe, I'd love to scoop you up and carry you in, but I *will* throw my back out trying to get you out of the car. It's too low." I nod sleepily and unbuckle, letting him take my hand and pull me up and out. Without really thinking about it, I wrap my arms around his neck and hop up a little to wrap my legs around his hips, burying my head against his neck. Without a word, he supports my butt with his arms and walks us into the elevator.

"Babe, can you grab your keys for me?" It's not easy, but I eventually wiggle them out by the time the elevator reaches our floor. Jason gets us inside and heads straight to my room. "You ready for bed?" I nod, feeling so tired that speaking is too much. He chuckles quietly, "Alright, sleepy head, arms up." He removes my top, then turns around and finds my PJs on top of my dresser. When he turns back, my bralette is off too, and he almost can't look away. I vaguely feel a little excited as he stares, my skin starting to feel hot and cold at the same time. If I wasn't so sleepy, I'd ask him to touch me, but my eyes feel like lead, and I don't think I'll be able to stay conscious enough to enjoy a little sexy time. Quickly, as if there's a fire, he gets me into my PJs and in bed. Before he can leave, I snag his hand in mine. "Stay."

He hesitates a moment, then nods. "I can do that; let me go lock up quick. I'll be right back." He can't have been gone for longer than thirty seconds, but I'm barely conscious when he returns. He shucks his jeans and shirt before joining me in bed. On instinct, I turn over and lay my head on his chest, hooking my leg over his. In response, he wraps both arms around me, gently stroking my back. I fall asleep listening to his heartbeat, a smile on my face.

CHAPTER 14

JASON

I wake up to find we've shifted. I'm spooning Alexis as if it were my job. Which, honestly, now, it kind of is. She's still asleep, her deep breaths the only sound. I peek around and find Slinky at the foot of the bed, curled against my legs. The clock reads eight-o-two. It's Sunday, and we both have no plans. It's so peaceful; I could just lay here forever.

My boner, however, would love to get taken care of.

I consider my options briefly. I could wake Alexis up and have a lil' morning fooling around. But we also didn't discuss where our boundaries are with sex yet, and I don't want to assume what she's comfortable with. So really, my only option is to get out of this magical bed and beat it off in the shower. I suppress a groan; I do not want to leave this bed.

Before I can make a move, though, Alexis turns over, slinging both an arm and a leg over my body. Now my poor dick is lined up right where it wants to be. I want to cry.

"Don't you dare get out of this bed." Her raspy sleep voice breaks the silence. *Thank fuck, she's awake.* She rubs her eyes and yawns before looking up at me with a shy smile. "Good morning."

"Good morning." I brush my thumb across her cheek, tracing a line of faint freckles. "Sleep well?" She nods against my chest, then plants a smacking kiss on my left pec, right over my heart. Before I quite realize what is happening, she's trailing kisses down my chest and abs, aiming straight for my briefs.

"Hey, whoa, you do not need to do that. Wait— fuck," one of her hands is already gripping me through the fabric, making my hips involuntarily push up from the bed. "Alexis, I'm serious. You do not need to worry about my morning wood."

She looks up, mouth hovering where I desperately want it, but know I shouldn't. "Jason, how about you worry about how good I'm about to make you feel rather than whether I want to suck your cock." Fuck. Me. "I wouldn't be doing this if I didn't want to."

How can any man argue with that?

Looking pleased as punch, she peels down my briefs, exposing my aching dick to the air. When she legit licks her lips in anticipation, I officially stop worrying about how this looks. Normally, I make sure the women I'm with orgasm at least once before I do, but she looks so excited to suck me off that there is literally nothing I'd be willing to do to stop her at this point.

She takes me in both hands first, firmly pumping me, making me groan loudly. "Fuck, baby, that feels so good." She smiles wickedly, and I know she's thinking she's about to make it feel even better.

She starts by dragging her tongue from root to tip, along the underside. I nearly come just from that. She does it again, chuckling like the vixen she is when I curse and grab the headboard for support. After sufficiently teasing me, she takes me into her hot, wet mouth. My eyes legitimately roll into the back of my head. It feels like heaven. "Shit, Lex, don't stop. That's right, take me as far as you can. Fuuuuuuck." When she hums around my dick, I lose all control, though.

"Alexis, baby, sit up," She protests as I ease her up, "Babe, I will let you get back to that, I promise, but I can't just lay here and let you have all the fun. Take your pants off." Half a beat passes, then I see it click. Did I wake up thinking I'd be 69-ing my new girlfriend? No. Is this the best morning of my life? Quite possibly.

She shimmies out of her PJ pants, and I help her get her sweet pussy over my face, her head back at my cock. Thank fuck, she's just tall enough.

She's already drenched when I press my tongue against her clit. She moans in response, and I can't help but palm her ass cheeks, gripping them hard. She rocks against my tongue gently, then fits me back in her mouth. I'm barely able to keep my hips on the bed. I'm not small, and I don't want to choke her on accident.

I first give her a few languorous licks along her entire slit before concentrating on her clit. One hand still gripping her ass, I hook the other arm around and sink one finger into her incredibly slick entrance. Her hips move jerkily against my face, and when I add a second finger, she moans loudly around my cock.

Her head is bobbing fast, and I can feel the beginnings of my orgasm in my balls. But I'm determined to get her there first. Two fingers pumping fast, I flutter my tongue on her clit, then suck on it hard. I repeat the flutter and suck combo a few more times before she suddenly comes, hard. I can feel her inner muscles spasming around my fingers, her cries muffled by my dick in her mouth. Fuck, that's sexy.

She doesn't stop her ministrations, though, even through her own orgasm. And within seconds, I'm coming. I barely have time to warn her before I'm seized by the hardest orgasm of my life. And no matter how much of a progressive dude I am, I can't help but be supremely satisfied as she swallows down every. Fucking. Drop.

She releases me with a pop and rolls off. We both lay there for a moment, catching our breaths. Her legs are still by my head, so I gently reach over and stroke her calves. That was amazing.

Our post-orgasm bliss is rudely interrupted when my phone goes off like crazy.

"I would really like to ignore that, but it sounds like I've just received a hundred messages." I groan and sit up. I can't help but smile as I reach for my phone because Alexis still looks blissed out, puffy lips and messy hair, wearing nothing but her PJ top. Before I turn my attention away, I lean down and give her a kiss.

Then I look at my phone.

"Shit." I open the first link and read the article title. "Fuck!"

Alexis sits up, worry creasing her brow. "What? What is it?" I just turn my phone over to her, so mad I can barely speak.

SPOTTED: JASON ADAMS AND MYSTERY WOMAN WERE SEEN AT

COUNTY FAIR LOOKING COZY – AND IN DIS-GUISE?

She sucks in a gasp, scrolling down, reading the article, and looking at the pictures. "How did they know we were there? I didn't even see anyone with a camera pointed at us!"

"Hell, if I know. Goddammit, we couldn't have even one outing?" I growl and get out of bed, quickly donning my clothes. "I'm going to grab us some breakfast, and we can talk about what we want to do in response. I'll be right back, ok?" She nods, still scrolling the article. I kiss the top of her head and leave. I quickly stopped for fresh clothes at my unit and grabbed my baseball hat and sunglasses.

Luckily, no one looks at me twice while grabbing pastries and coffee, so I'm back to Alexis' in record time. She's out of bed, changed into a sundress, and is already on the balcony waiting for me.

"Here's your phone back. I don't know if you saw, but they even caught a picture of us making out on the Ferris Wheel. There is pretty much no hiding things now."

I take a seat next to her and take a moment to think. Sipping my coffee, I reach out and take her hand in mine, rubbing my thumb over the back of her hand.

"Ok, so I think if we go public, maybe post something on my Instagram and then have a statement put out tomorrow, things will calm down. Do you think you're ready for that?"

She turns to look at me, a sad smile on her face. "Do you really think it will help? Won't it just add more fuel to the fire?"

"I wish I could say with certainty that things will die down after, but I can't. In my experience, though, the longer you wait to address things like that, the more people decide their own narrative and just make shit up." I sigh, wishing my life wasn't in the public eye so much. Wishing I had done something else with my life. What if all of this is too much for her?

Just as I feel myself start to spiral, Alexis' hand squeezes mine.

"Honestly, I don't think I'll ever be ready for that, but it's basically out of our hands already. Next time, they might find me at the hospital and start harassing people there. I don't even want to think about what the hospital will do if that happens. I could lose my job for all I know. I'm not going to pretend that this doesn't scare me, but I think it's time to take control of the narrative. And now." I nod. I completely agree. An apology is on the tip of my tongue, but I bite it back; it won't help things now.

"Alright, I agree. Come here." I have her get onto my lap crossways and snap a few selfies. I post my two favorites, one where she smiles at the camera with me and one where she's kissing me on the cheek. I look like a happy man in both, and honestly, despite the media shitstorm, I am.

I add the caption "cats out of the bag" and tag her. I hope she realizes she's going to get hundreds of follow requests.

We both turn off the volume on our phones and spend the rest of the day just enjoying each other's company.

Chapter 15

Alexis

"How's my sweet girl?" My mom's voice crackles over my car speakers. Her connection must not be great; she and my dad are somewhere in Brazil at the moment.

"Hi, Mom. Hi, Dad! I'm almost to the hospital, so I can't talk long." I'm actually about forty minutes from work, but they don't know that. I love my parents, but they love to chat, and I'm just not in the mood right now.

Jason's official statement was released two days ago, detailing our relationship as vaguely as possible while still sating the appetite of everyone looking for information. We made the request that my privacy be respected, and except for a few people at work asking if it's true, it seems like I'm being left alone. At least when I'm by myself. When I'm out with Jason, though? We aren't often left alone. Jason's spent every night with me since Sunday, but he left this morning for on-location filming. I won't see him until this upcoming Saturday. He's taking me to a charity auction as our first official outing. I am equal parts excited and terrified.

"No worries at all, my little turtle dove; your father and I have a snorkel lesson in a few minutes anyway. We just wanted to check-in. We've seen some photos online, and a few friends have sent us some articles with you in them... is there something you want to tell us?"

I stifle a groan. She's using the tone of voice that says *I know you're keeping secrets; I know what they are, but I'm giving you a chance to fess up before I rip you a new one.* I don't think I've heard this particular voice since I was thirteen. Well, as Jason said, the cat's out of the bag. No sense in pretending.

"Mom, don't give me that tone. I'm nearly thirty. I am allowed some privacy these days. That being said, the articles are true. Jason Adams and I are dating." Her squeals of delight cut me off. Oh boy. "Mom. Mom, please stop. Can I please finish?" I can hear my dad in the background telling her to calm down and let me continue. I love my dad. He stabilizes her crazy.

"Ok, honey, I'm sorry. I've just been worried about you since your father and I are globe-trotting, and you're in L.A. all alone. I just want you to be happy. Are you happy?" She sounds so hopeful. I can almost guarantee that if I saw her eyes right now, there would be babies in them. She covets grandmahood like no other.

"I am happy. Jason lives in my building, and we met because of Slinky, actually. When you're home, we'll tell you the story in depth. It's a bit too long for right now. Anyway, we started out just as friends, but we both felt a connection. And then the media caught wind of us, and we had to decide what we wanted. They were making things up, and we had to set the record straight. So, we're dating. And yes, before you ask, you can meet him when you're home next."

She's nearly incoherent as she expresses her delight. She doesn't care one bit about his celebrity status, although I bet my father wouldn't mind an autograph or two. No, what has my mom excited is the possibility of a wedding and babies, and of course, her daughter's happiness. My parents had both been previously married before they met. Divorcées wholly disillusioned by the idea of love. Neither planned on the other when my mom's nephew ended up in the hospital after a bad car accident. My father was the pediatric surgeon on-call who treated my cousin. My mother was the pesky science teacher aunt who knew just a little too much about human anatomy and kept questioning him about her nephew's prognosis and recovery.

My father maintains to this day that he found my mother's tenacity and intelligence intriguing. My mother claims that they hated each other. Regardless, they eventually gave in to their mutual attraction and married. They struggled for years to have a child, and I came around when my mom was forty-one. Which is why they are both already fully retired, and I've barely even started my career. My apartment is actually theirs. They bought it when I started medical school and begged me to 'take care of it' while they traveled. They pretend I'm doing them a favor, but really, they bought this place so that I could live near my school and eventually my place of residency for free. I'll let them pretend, though.

"Mom, Dad, I'm pulling into the hospital parking lot," I'm really not. I have another twenty minutes, but they don't need to know that. "I'll talk to you soon, ya? Have fun snorkeling!"

"Ok, bye honey, have a good day at work. We love you!"

"Love you, sweetheart. Don't let any of the attendings push you around; you'll be one of them soon." I smile; that's my dad, behind my career 110 percent.

"Love you both, bye." I quickly hang up before they can say anything else. From experience, our goodbyes can last several minutes.

My shift was uneventful medicine-wise but filled with getting peppered with questions at every moment by Allison and Tristan, who have the same shift as me. Allison kept sneaking information to Nique via text, which was the only way we could convince her to stay home and enjoy her day off. These three are nuts.

"Lex, we're just glad you've found someone who treats you right. You spend so much time here or at your apartment, and we *know* it's been a while since you got any from anything other than your vibrator." Tristan hits me with a *come on, you know I'm right*, look. She and I managed to get our lunches scheduled together and are chatting in the cafeteria. I can almost hear Allison back in the ER fuming over the fact that she can't be here.

"Look, I get it. I'm obviously excited too. It's been a while since I've touched a penis beyond medical. But this is also incredibly new. I don't want to jinx us by talking like it's this big love story with a happy ending. We're having fun right now, and I don't want to pressure us." Tristan nods, hopefully in agreement. She's been the most level-headed about this new development in my life, so I'm hoping she'll calm down the rabid dogs that are Allison and Nique. Allison is already asking me if her kids can be my go-to babysitters when I pop out a few of my own. She's a little overzealous.

"I'll calm down Ally and Kiki for you, at least for now. But they'll want to have a total debrief soon. Especially if we keep seeing your picture in tabloid magazines." I groan. Yesterday morning, Jason and I got coffee before my shift, and some pap took our picture mid-kiss. It's been splashed all over the internet. We now have a couple name: Jaxis. Which first of all? Ew. Second of all? Sexist. Why does Jason's name get to go first? Couldn't they have picked something with our last names? Mastams? Fuck, no, that's not good either.

"Again, I get it. But the media has already blown this up so much that I can't take pressure from my friends too. I just... I just want to enjoy this while it lasts. Ok?"

"I hear you, loud and clear. I'll wrangle the other two in to-day." She reaches over and gives my hand a comforting squeeze. We pass the rest of our lunchtime talking about Tristan's old as dirt dog, Maestro.

Later that night, I'm carrying in the take-out I picked up on my way home when I nearly trip over a box sitting outside my door. I smile; I don't even have to look at the note to know who it's from.

Once I get everything inside and have my food in front of me, I pull out the card to read. This note is typed, probably because it was printed by the courier company who brought the box, so I'm not deciphering his awful handwriting for once.

Lexi,

I got you something for our night at the auction. I hope you like it. Please call my assistant though, if you need something different. The designer had several options, but I thought this one was the most you. Fingers crossed I got it right.

I already miss you, see you Saturday.

Your main squeeze, Jason

P.S. You won't hurt my feelings if this isn't your style. I want you to feel beautiful, and if this isn't right, try something else until you find the right one.

I suppress the lovestruck sigh that wants to escape my lips. That big goof bought me a dress. Before he left, I expressed a worry that I wouldn't have time to pick out a dress. I'm working ten-hour shifts every day, including the charity auction night. He's going to have to pick me up straight from the hospital. It seems he paid attention and took care of it for me. How in the hell is he this perfect?

I quickly slam the rest of my dinner, clean up and put away the leftovers, then bring the box into my bedroom to try on. I give an audible gasp when I open the box. I haven't even pulled it out, and already I know it's perfect.

The dress is to die for. Dark forest green velvet, with a high neck and long fitted sleeves. The skirt flows elegantly from the waist to the floor, with a slit that looks like it doesn't go too high. It's the back that makes it truly stunning, though. There's a strip of fabric at the back of the neck with two buttons, then nothing. The back is completely open until the small of my back.

I almost don't want to try it on in case I somehow manage the ruin it. But it needs to be done, just in case it doesn't fit. I shut my door, making sure Slinky is still out in the living room on her cat tree; I can't risk her making mischief just yet. I then strip down and step into the dress. Fits like a glove, as if there was any doubt.

Alexis: I love it, thank you. [heart emoji]

I feel so beautiful in this gown that I almost cry. The designer may have brought him the options, but Jason picked this dress for me. He found exactly what I would have chosen for myself without ever needing direction. If I needed a sign that the man seriously liked me, this is it. There are also shoes in the box that go with the dress, and they, of course, fit as well.

Jason: Glad you love it. I can't wait to see you Saturday. Sleep tight. xoxoxoxo

Saturday can't get here fast enough.

CHAPTER 16

JASON

I can barely keep my leg from jiggling the whole ride to the hospital. Alexis texted me about half an hour ago, saying she was nearly ready, and that was the exact moment I remembered something that I wish I hadn't forgotten.

Now I'm nervous as hell.

And not because this will be Alexis' first red carpet event or that we will spend a lot of our time mingling with people she's never met before.

Oh no.

No, I'm insanely anxious because I remembered why I got seats at this auction. My parents. More specifically, my mother is on their board of directors and had us purchase a table. So not only is my brand-new girlfriend unexpectedly meeting my parents, but she's also going to meet my sister, my sister's current boyfriend, and two sets of aunts and uncles. And I, being the dumbass I am, haven't prepared her at all.

I messed up, big time.

When the town car I got us for the evening rolls up to the hospital front entrance, I'm so nervous I might vomit into one of the concrete planters lining the sidewalk.

Just as I'm getting out to collect her, Alexis steps out.

Holy fuck.

I'm dead.

I make a note to get Slinky a lifetime supply of her favorite treats. Without her, I wouldn't be watching this goddess of a doctor walking toward me right now. She is radiant.

When I reached out to my friend, Mei-Ling, for a favor, I knew she'd hook me up, but I didn't understand just how amazing Alexis would look in the dress until now. The fitted velvet bodice and sleeves fit her like a second skin. The skirt flows like water around her legs, with one popping out occasionally through the slit. As she gets closer, I twirl my finger around, asking to see the back. She blushes and gives me a spin, giggling the whole time. Fuck me, the back. Equal parts sexy and elegant. Now I'm cursing at the fact that we need to get to the venue soon because the caveman inside of me really wants to find a quiet spot where I can eat her out in this dress. I take in her makeup and hair when she's finally in front of me. Nique nicely stayed after her shift to help Alexis get dressed and do her hair and makeup. It's the perfect mix of Hollywood glam and Alexis. I take her face between my hands, careful not to touch her updo, and kiss her like my life depends on it.

Her hands come to my chest, grabbing the lapels of my tux. At the contact, my dick gets heavy, and I know I have to pull away before we have a problem.

"You are fucking stunning."

"You're pretty handsome yourself tonight. This tux? It's doing things to me." She huffs a laugh, then adds, "are you sure we need to go? I wouldn't mind skipping and doing something different tonight."

I turn and open the town car door for her and urge her in. "As much as I would love that, I do really need to go tonight."

I climb in behind her, then take her hand, absently rubbing my thumb along the back. This is quickly becoming my favorite thing. Just sitting with her quietly, holding one of her hands.

"I do have to tell you something, though." I give her a sheepish look, hoping she doesn't ask to be dropped off at home after I break the news. "I kind of forgot what this was for. I sign up for these sometimes so far in advance that they all blend together. But uh, this particular charity event is put on by a foundation that my mom is on the board of... so you'll be meeting my parents tonight." I wince, knowing this isn't the best situation in the world. She opens her mouth to say something, but I cut her off to get the rest out. "Annnd, it won't just be my parents. We're sitting at a table with my sister, her boyfriend, my two aunts, and their husbands. If you want to go home, I would completely understand. I did not mean to ambush you with basically my entire family."

I look away, not ready to see whatever is on her face. When she squeezes my hand, I force myself to look at her, and all I see is mild amusement.

"Jason, do I wish I'd had a little more notice? Sure. Am I going to rip you a new one over this? No. Because in a month, I get to return the favor when *my* parents come home for a bit and will live in my apartment with me. Get ready, buddy, because my mom *will* ask you five times a day when you're going to marry me and start having kids."

I let out the breath I've been holding and chuckle a bit. Her mom sounds a lot like mine.

"Let's just try to enjoy ourselves tonight and not worry about your parents or mine. Sound good?"

"Sounds perfect."

She then lays her head on my shoulder, and we relax quietly for the rest of the ride. I've learned that Alexis enjoys and often needs quiet time. And the more we do it together, the more I look forward to it too. There's something about being with someone you care about and just enjoying their company, no expectations or obligations, just being in their presence. It soothes the soul.

The red carpet is in full swing when we pull up to the venue. There are a few cars ahead of us, so we have time before entering the chaos.

"Ok, so I'm going to step out, then I'll help you out. We'll head down the carpet and get a few requests to stop, answer some questions, and pose for a few photos. Just remember you don't have to say anything if the question makes you uncomfortable. Mostly I think people will ask you about what you're wearing and what you do."

She looks out the windows, chewing her lip nervously. My chest grows tight at her expression. I touch her cheek gently, bringing her attention back.

"Just remember, I'll be with you the whole time, and if you want to keep moving, just let me know. Speaking of your dress, it was made by a friend of mine, Mei-Ling. She was an assistant costume director on a few of my movies, and some of her original pieces got used. Her tailoring is impeccable, so I commissioned a few suits and tuxes from her and then helped her start her brand when she was ready. She mostly does this on the side, but she wants to do it full-time, so tonight will be a good way to show off her pieces. She made this tux too."

Alexis nods, rubbing her hand along the skirt of her dress with appreciation. I know that she'll be telling every reporter who made this dress tonight that she never passes on an opportunity to help someone.

This feeling in my chest won't go away. I know what it is, but I'm not sure I'm ready to give it a name. All I know is that Alexis has very quickly become the center of my world. And I never want to lose that.

We finally reach the spot where we get out, and I turn and give her a reassuring smile. "You are radiant tonight, and anyone who tries to make you feel small is only doing it because they're jealous. You ready?"

She gives me a shaky nod, and I let one of the event staff open the door. The sounds of red-carpet chaos flood the car, and she stiffens next to me. I step out, waving to the people screaming my name. Then I reach back and help her out.

If I thought the crowd was excited to see me, I was wrong. The second people realize who it is that I am helping out of the car, they go *wild*.

She turns to me wide-eyed, "Is it always like this for you?" I can't help but laugh; she doesn't realize that she's become a sensation over the last few weeks. "Sometimes, but tonight, babe? This is all for you." I tuck her hand into the crook of my elbow and begin our walk down the carpet.

At our first stop, a switch seems to flip, and Alexis morphs into a veteran of the carpet. We end up stopping often, posing together, or even sometimes just Alexis herself, showing off her dress. At every opportunity, she hypes Mei-Ling up, just like I knew she would. The best is when the questions get a little too invasive. Her token reply the whole time was, "That's between me and Jason, but thank you for your curiosity." She's so gracious that the reporters don't even realize they've been brushed off until we move on. Honestly, by the time we get to the doors, I'm decoration. I love it.

We're taking our last photo before we head in. Alexis is looking at the camera, but I can't keep my eyes off her. She's the best thing to happen to me in a long time, and that pesky L-word keeps clamoring to get out. *We aren't there yet. Calm down.* But boy, do I want to be.

We finally make it to our table, and my parents and sister immediately pounce. I cut my mom a look that says *don't overwhelm her.* My mom just smiles back at me as if she has no idea what my expression means. Fuck me.

"Alexis! I am so glad you could make it tonight! I'm Martha, Jason's mother. This is Thomas, my husband, and Isla, my youngest." Alexis sticks out her hand to shake theirs and is immediately foiled when my mom pulls her in for a big hug. Like I said, my mom is very loving, if a little pushy.

"Hi, Mrs. Adams, Mr. Adams, Isla. It's so nice to meet you all." I have to laugh because Alexis is doing her best to get out of the stranglehold my mom has on her, but she won't let go. Finally, my mom pulls back, keeping her hands on Alexis' arms to take in her dress.

"Alexis dear, none of that Mrs. and Mr. crap. Tom and I don't stand on ceremony ever. And I have to tell you, honey, your dress is stunning. Who designed it?"

With the ice broken, we're able to give Mei-Ling another plug and settle at the table. Shortly after, the dinner service starts along with the presentations. The auction will be held at the end. This charity raises money a few times a year to help fund struggling pediatric cancer wards. It's always a huge celebrity event because you can never get enough good PR when helping fund kids' cancer treatment. Isla had childhood leukemia and is fine now, but my parents care deeply about helping other children survive and thrive after cancer. And as soon as I had enough money to donate to charities, I followed in their foot-steps. Giving back is another thing we, as the Adamses just do.

I spend the whole dinner with at least one hand on Alexis at all times. She's seated next to my sister, and they seem to get along. Once or twice, she'll reach down and give my knee a squeeze. Everything about tonight just feels natural. Easy.

I can see my mom across the table watching us; she looks me directly in the eye at one point, then points to her ring finger. *Marry her*, she mouths. Trust me, I'm thinking about it. Luckily, Alexis is deep in conversation with Isla and doesn't notice this exchange. I know she's felt a lot of pressure since this all started, and I don't want her to think she's getting it from my family too.

Once dessert is served, tonight's auctioneer gets up on stage to get the fun part rolling.

I lean over to Alexis, getting her full attention for the first time since we sat down. "If you see anything you're interested in bidding on, just let me know. There are usually a few things worth dropping some cash on."

She shakes her head, scrunching her nose. "Oh no, you don't. I know how much these seats cost. I'm not spending any more of your money tonight. I'm happy just to be here with you and your family."

I laugh, rolling my eyes. "Seriously, I have a good sum set aside for this event. If you don't pick something, I'll just have to bid on something random." She just rolls her eyes and turns back to my sister. If we weren't in public, I'd pull her into my lap and tickle her until she cries mercy. She's so ticklish she can barely last five seconds before giving in. It would be so easy.

The microphone crackles over the sound system, and the crowd quiets down. "Ladies, gentlemen, and honored guests. Thank you very much for attending the tenth annual Lee Church Foundation Auction. First, on the docket, tonight is everyone's favorite. We have five wonderful bachelors offering up a lunch date for the lucky highest bidder. Can I get all five men up on stage with me, please?"

"Fuck." I turn to my mom, who looks like a cat in cream. She one-hundred percent remembered this was happening tonight and is enjoying my moment of tortured realization.

Alexis hears my curse and looks at me, confused.

I kiss her quick on the lips and smile apologetically. "I'm sorry, babe. I'll make it right, though." She still looks confused as I get up, re-button my tux, and head toward the stage with four other men.

How the hell did I also forget this?

Easy, my mind has been occupied by a certain hot doctor the past few weeks.

Chapter 17

Alexis

Isla and I are having a great time getting to know each other tonight. I won't lie; I was so nervous about meeting his family. But they've been nothing but welcoming and genuinely interested in me as a person, not Jason's arm candy.

So, when Jason heads toward the stage, blood drained from his face, looking like he's about to face his worst enemy; she and I burst into laughter.

She and I are going to get along swimmingly.

I can't help but watch his every move as he joins the other men on stage. I may be biased, but he is the best-looking one up there. I wonder how much a lunch with him will go for? I briefly consider using his paddle and bidding for him, but no. Letting him suffer through this is too good. I'm secure enough in our relationship to know that this is for charity, and while he would be nice to whoever wins the bid, he'll make it clear that nothing will come of it.

He's second in line, and I can't help but laugh again; he looks so miserable. While the other guys are smiling and winking at the crowd, clearly trying to pump them up, my poor man just looks like he wants to disappear.

The first guy's date goes for five thousand, which honestly seemed low to me. As the auctioneer comes to Jason, he goes up to the podium and clearly requests the mic. The auctioneer is confused at first, but hands it over reluctantly. I sit up straight, wondering what the hell he is doing.

"Hello, everyone, you may know me already, but I'm Jason Adams. I was super single when I signed up for this months ago, but in case you've been living under a rock, I recently started dating the lovely Dr. Alexis Masters." He points to me, and a spotlight quickly spins around and lights me up. I blush, smiling shyly at the crowd, who are now all looking at me. I wave and get a friendly chuckle from the guests. "So, unfortunately, all my lunches are spoken for. I'll be donating ten thousand, though, to compensate for any loss by me stepping down. Have a good night, everyone."

He steps off stage, aiming straight for me, cool as a cucumber. The crowd has dissolved into whispers and quiet laughter. This will absolutely be in every gossip magazine tomorrow.

When he finally gets back to our table, he tips my head back for a kiss that lasts much longer than is socially acceptable. When he breaks our kiss, I'm in a daze, suddenly wishing we were home. He retakes his seat and drags mine closer, wrapping an arm around me and giving me another kiss on my temple. I can't help but peek at his parents across the table. Martha is watching us with hearts in her eyes, while Tom is clearly still laughing over his son's antics.

"You did not need to do that, you know." I pull back to see his face, pinching his chin and rolling my eyes. "My ego can handle you taking someone out to lunch for charity."

He smiles and pinches my chin right back, the bastard. "Oh, I know, but why suffer through a potentially boring lunch when I could donate to a good cause and focus my energy on spending time with you? Now pay attention to the rest of the auction. We're not leaving tonight until I bid and win something for you."

An hour later, we're saying our goodbyes. Jason won a sunset dinner cruise on a sailboat after a fierce bidding war with some old dude. Seriously, I thought they were going to start fighting. They were giving each other such murderous stares. Finally, the guy's wife whispered in his ear, and he gave up.

"Mom, please tell the staff and the board that tonight was wonderful. You all outdid yourselves as usual." Jason hugs his mom close, then moves to chat with his dad and sister.

Martha approaches me and takes my hand. "I hope this isn't too invasive of me, but I've been watching you and my son all night, and I see how much you care for each other. Am I jumping the gun by hoping there'll be wedding bells soon?" She looks so hopeful and happy that I hesitate to crush her dreams. She and my mom will get along just fine. It's almost comical how similar they are.

"Martha, I'll be honest, I care for your son deeply. But we've only just started our relationship, so no, we aren't getting married soon. When we do make that next step, you'll be the first to know." She nods, accepting my answer, and we hug goodbye.

Isla and I make plans for coffee, which I can see makes Jason nervous. He doesn't want us ganging up on him. Little does he know we're already well on our way to being a team against him.

After what feels like an eternity later, we're back in the town car. As soon as he's seated, Jason puts up the privacy shade between the driver and us and pulls me into his lap. "Those goodbyes felt like an eternity. My mom didn't say anything she shouldn't, did she?" I shake my head and press my mouth to his. We spend the rest of the car ride making out like a couple of teenagers.

By the time we reach our building, I am on fire. Up until tonight, we've got each other off with hands and mouths, but tonight he is going to rail me properly. I won't let him stop us.

My center aches for him, and I'm already soaked.

I manage to keep it together until we're in the elevator alone. I turn to Jason, handing over my keys, and say, "Jason, if you don't fuck me until I forget my name tonight, I will not be happy."

"Babe, you read my mind." He yanks me into his arms and helps me adjust my skirt so I can wrap my legs around his waist. Thank you, Mei-Ling, for adding a slit! Our lips are practically fused together, tongues dancing as he presses me against one of the elevator walls and grinds against me. I can't help but gasp when our centers line up. If this is exquisite, how will it feel when he's finally inside of me?

The elevator dings, and we, well Jason, stumble out, one arm holding me up, the other fumbling with my keys.

To say I have never been so desperate to have sex with someone in my life would be a gross understatement.

Finally, we're in my unit, and clothes start to come off. Shoes first, then his bow tie and jacket. By the time we reach my room, his shirt is half off and pants unzipped. But we're struggling with my dress.

"Fuck, babe, I'm going to have to put you down. I can't see what I'm doing, and these buttons aren't cooperating. If I didn't think Mei-Ling would castrate me, I would just rip them."

"No! Don't do that. I love this dress. Put me down." He sets me down, and I turn so he can see what he's doing. A minute later, my dress sags forward, and I can start peeling it off. As it pools at my feet, I turn to find Jason staring slack-jawed. He didn't expect me to be completely naked underneath that dress. He groans, trailing a finger down my chest, gently tugging one nipple, making me gasp. "Damn, Alexis, it is a good thing I didn't know you weren't wearing panties. I would have had my hand up your skirt all night."

He pulls me close for another searing kiss, and we work together to get the rest of his clothes off. We both moan when our naked bodies finally meet. With little effort, he picks me up again and tosses me onto my bed. I can't help but giggle in anticipation.

He stands there a moment, stroking himself. I bite my lip, suddenly wishing my mouth and hands were doing that instead. "Nope, not yet, Doctor. I have plans for you that don't involve you sucking my dick just yet." He smiles wickedly, and my center clenches in anticipation. I am *so ready* for whatever he wants. "Reach behind and grab your headboard with both hands. You aren't allowed to let go of it until you come. Do you understand?"

"Yes," my voice sounds breathy; I'm already on the edge. Holy shit, he's going to end me. I grab the headboard, and he finally joins me on the bed. He starts at my lips again, then trails biting kisses along my jaw, down the side of my neck. He spends an extra moment at the spot where my shoulder meets my neck. I've never enjoyed a hickey so much in my life, my back arching off the bed at the feel of his mouth sucking on my skin. Hard.

By the time he makes it to my breasts, I'm a mess. I'm aching and so close to coming, I feel crazy. "Jason! Fuck, please just fuck me, baby. I'm so close."

He tuts at me, shaking his head before pulling one of my breasts into his mouth, swirling his tongue around my already hard nipple. My hips move on their own, trying to find release. But I'm foiled by Jason, who plants a hand on my hip, pinning me to the bed.

"You'll come soon, Lex, I promise. But right now, I'm going to worship your tits like I've wanted to all night."

He moves on to the other and gives it the same ministrations. My fingers itch to plunge into his hair or scrape down his back. But he gave me an order, and I can't seem to disobey.

I let out a shriek when he introduces his teeth, gently tugging on my nipple. He moves back and forth, sending me into a state of near hysteria. "Jason, Jason, Jason."

I nearly cry in relief as his lips move south, my legs instantly dropping open. I'm desperate for him to finish me off. Both his hands move up to palm and pinch my breasts. I'm practically bucking him off with my need to come.

He looks up at me from between my legs, and I see the twinkle in his eyes before he gently blows cool air against my clit. I moan so loudly; I know my neighbors can hear me. He doesn't make me wait any longer; as soon as I relax back down, his mouth descends on my clit, and he sucks hard.

I'm off the bed like a shot, coming so hard I don't even make noise. Stars are bursting behind my eyelids. Holy shit, I've never come so hard on basically only nipple play. Is he a god?

He's gently licking my slit, lapping up my arousal that is now flooding my center. "That feel good?" I gasp and slap his hand; *did that feel good*? The audacity of this man.

"Jason, that was the best orgasm of my life. Don't pretend to be humble. Condom, now."

He sits up quickly, going into my nightstand, where a fresh box of condoms waits. He rolls one on in record time and quickly gets into position between my legs.

"Alexis, baby, I'm so close. This is going to be quick and hard, ok?" I nod urgently, pulling his head down by his hair. "You better make me see stars again, Hollywood," I say against his lips. His response is to growl and enters me with a powerful thrust.

My eyes roll back in my head, and we both moan. He fills me up so tight. It feels so good; tears leak out of the corner of my eyes.

Then he pumps, hard and fast, and I swear I ascend to another plane of existence. I scrape my fingers down his back, earning another satisfied growl. My legs are hooked around his, so I can plant my feet and meet his thrusts. My fingers dig into his ass, urging him to pump faster, harder. His pelvis keeps hitting my clit, creating exquisite friction. He thrusts his own fingers into my hair, trapping my mouth in place while his tongue mimics his lower body. Within minutes, we have to break the seal of our lips to cry out in pleasure. He shouts my name as he comes, and

I let out another silent scream, coming so hard I can feel myself clench around him.

"Shit, Alexis, that was – " he slumps over, barely able to speak coherently, "that was amazing." We're both breathing hard, still coming down. My hands can't stop running up and down his back, reveling in the layer of sweat we created. After another moment, he gently pulls out and rolls to the side, dragging me with him, so I'm snuggled into his chest.

"I need to get rid of this condom, but I don't want to move." I nod, unable to think of a single word in the English language.

I'm not sure how long we lay there, but finally, my bladder makes an appearance. I sit up, and Jason follows. He follows me directly into the bathroom, not giving a single damn that I'm peeing in front of him while he removes the condom and ties it off.

I finish up, then stand at the sink to wash my hands. I watch Jason through the mirror as he steps behind me, leisurely dragging his hands up my sides, gently massaging my shoulders before starting to pull the pins out of my hair. I sigh in relief, my scalp prickling, as he lets down my hair. I didn't even realize it was bothering me until now. With the pins out, he switches between finger combing the curls and massaging my scalp. I can't help but drop my head back against his chest and moan. "That feels so good." My eyes flutter closed.

"Hmmm, everything about you feels good." He turns me around and then sits me up on the counter. "Where's your stuff to take your makeup off?" I slow blink at him, not quite computing what he says at first.

"Oh, um, I use a bottle of micellar water and cotton makeup pads in that cabinet." He digs through my cabinet and pulls out what he needs. I tell him to soak the pad and concentrate on my face first, then my eyelids. I close my eyes while he diligently wipes away the sweat and makeup, feeling almost overwhelmed by this need to let him take care of me.

When he's done, he picks me up off the counter and brings me back to bed. After we settle against each other comfortably, it takes almost no effort for me to drift off. *This* is what it means to find belonging with someone.

CHAPTER 18

JASON

Last night, fuck, last night was everything.

We slept for maybe an hour before I woke to Alexis sucking my soul through my dick. I nearly shouted the L-word twice.

And now we're spooning again in the early morning light, and I can barely handle how much I feel for her. I can't hold it in.

She's still asleep, so it's easier as I whisper, "I love you," between kisses along her hairline and shoulder. She starts to stir as I trail one hand up and down her chest in a sloppy figure eight, barely grazing the innermost edges of her tits. Usually, I'm an ass man, and hers absolutely sends me, but her tits? Something about them being just big enough to fit the palm of my hand and the dusky pink hue of her nipples makes me all twisted up.

I grow the figure eight so that one loop spans across the top of her chest and collarbone, passing between her breasts. The bottom loop travels over the top of her stomach, grazing the underside of her breasts. She's still sleeping, but her nipples are hard as diamonds. I bet it would already be wet if I felt between her legs. For now, though, I'm content with just teasing her body until she wakes.

Finally, her eyes flutter open, and she sighs, pressing her ass against my already hard cock. I groan into her hair and press my hips forward, sliding my length through her ass cheeks. She moans in response. I shift the arm she's been using as a pillow around her shoulders, pressing her upper half against my chest. Her head turns toward me just enough so I can capture her lips in mine. She whimpers, shifting her body so that it fits tightly against mine. I know what she wants, and I'll give it to her.

With my free hand, I trace little circles down her torso, leaving goosebumps in my wake. Her hips shift as my hand slides between her legs. I stay at her clit for a few minutes, slowly circling one blunt finger. She breaks our kiss to moan and throws her head back against my shoulder. I take the opportunity to bite down on her shoulder, eliciting another sweet moan. At this point, my dick is throbbing, begging to be inside her. So far, we haven't said anything, just communicated through sighs, moans, and touches. When my hand leaves her clit and grazes her slick center, she nods frantically, breaths coming quick.

I take her top leg and position it over my own, giving me just enough room to slide in. We both groan as the underside of my dick rubs against her G-spot. I can't go as deep as I want in this position, but it still feels amazing. There's no rush; the goal is to enjoy each other, not race to the finish line. I use long, languorous strokes to stoke her fire patiently. Once she's panting heavily, I kick it up a notch, reciting the titles of every movie I've been in to keep myself from coming too soon. My hand goes back to her clit, strumming it firmly. One of her hands comes to the back of my head, threading her fingers through my hair, the other clutches my hand at her clit, pressing it firmer against her.

"Jason!" she cries out as she comes suddenly. The feel of her inner muscles clenching and releasing around me sets off my orgasm. As I groan out her name, my teeth sink into her neck.

We both come down slowly. It's only when she shifts to get a better angle to kiss me again that I slip out and realize something we both forgot. "Shit."

"What? What's wrong?" She turns more fully, alarmed. I smooth a hand over her brow to reassure her. "I'm so sorry, Alexis. I forgot a condom. I was just so caught up in making you feel good, I didn't think."

I flop on my back, furious with myself. I've never once gone without one. While kids are definitely a possibility in the future, I know Alexis and I aren't there yet; hell, we've only just started dating. As I begin to spiral, she does the exact opposite. I almost think I'm going crazy when I hear her laugh. I sit up and look down at her incredulously; how is she being chill about this?

She smiles at me, throwing an arm over her eyes. "I'm sorry, Hollywood. I don't mean to laugh at you. I just know that we're safe. I have an IUD and just finished my period, so I'm at the stage in my cycle when I'm least likely to get pregnant. We can go to the pharmacy to get Plan B if you want to be extra safe. But as a doctor, I feel comfortable saying we're good." She pauses, reaching up and pinching my chin, "but next time, let's remember the condom. Sound ok?"

I flop back down on the bed and laugh. I went from post-orgasm high to pregnancy panic, back down to normal in like sixty seconds. I'm reeling a bit, to be honest.

"While I am very glad you aren't worried about it, it brings up a question." I shift back on my side so that I'm facing her. She rolls to do the same. I reach out and take her hand, interlacing her fingers with mine. "I don't know about you, but my feelings for you have gotten serious pretty quickly. And if you're not at the same place, that's totally fine, but I need you to know where I am at." I chance a glance at her face and see hesitation. Shit. She's not on the same page. My gut roils, feeling like I revealed too much too fast.

I go to pull away, suddenly feeling like I need to leave. But her hand clamps down on mine with strength I did not know she possessed.

"You are not leaving this bed before I say what I need to say." I nod and settle back in, my heart beating wildly in my chest.

"I've never been in a serious relationship before. I've dated a few men, mostly in college and med school, but they were never serious. I always knew they were temporary, and so did they. But with you... it's completely different. I guess what I am trying to say is that this thing between us is serious for me too. And." She hesitates, worrying her bottom lip between her teeth.

She takes a deep breath, then looks up into my eyes, and I see it. Shining through before she even says anything. "I love you too."

"You do? Wait, you heard me? Earlier?" She nods, leaning in to kiss me quickly.

"I did, and I don't feel bad for pretending to still be sleeping." I can't help but smile, giving her my own quick kiss. Damn, I love her.

"I love you," I say, kissing her again. "I love you; I love you; I love you." It's as if a dam has been broken, now that I've said it. I can't stop. She giggles in response as I continue to pepper her with kisses, tugging her down under me.

"WAIT!" I pull back, wondering what else she could say. She smiles mischievously. "Grab a condom, and I love you." She squeals loudly as I begin to tickle her mercilessly, she knows better than to tease me like that.

Hours later, we're still in bed, though we have managed to shower, change the sheets, and give Slinky some attention. We're both currently propped up, reading quietly together, Slinky curled up in the space between us. At this moment, I see us twenty years in the future. We'll be older, a bit wiser, maybe a few grays, but we'll be happy.

I look forward to it.

Chapter 19

Alexis

We get three blissful days of peace after the gala before all hell breaks loose.

Honestly, I can't believe it took them as long as it did to nearly tear it all down. There was always going to be a shoe to drop.

"I'm headed out!" I call from the doorway, barely catching Jason's muffled goodbye from my bed. I can't stop the self-satisfied smirk that creeps across my face as I lock up. Despite having to wake up way too early for my shift today, I enjoyed making Jason a babbling idiot before leaving. Nothing like leaving your boyfriend incoherent from pleasure to start your workday off right.

The drive to the hospital is thankfully quick and uneventful. At this time of day, or is it night? Either way, at this point, L.A. traffic is at its lightest, which means my commute is reasonable. I make it to the hospital in record time.

After a brief pit stop at the locker room, I head out onto the ER floor and take a deep breath, centering myself for the day. As a fourth-year resident, this is my time to shine. To show my superiors that not only do I have the academics required to practice medicine, but I have the skills too. My entire future hangs on how I finish this year, and it's as scary as it sounds. All eyes are on me, and I can't let myself or my family down. Not this time.

Despite having a pleasant morning with Jason and doing all my normal pre-shift routines, I still feel vaguely anxious. There's a tight ball under my ribcage that just won't ease, no matter how many belly breaths I take.

Ignoring the feeling, I concentrate as one of my nurses explains the head trauma case I'm seeing first. It takes a few minutes, but eventually, I'm able to sink into my doctor brain and block everything else.

***

"Uh, Doctor?" I glance up from the X-Rays I'm pulling up onto the screen and glance over at the lanky soccer player on the table. Her demeanor is completely different from when I first came in. She went from a frustrated but confident player hoping her foot wasn't broken, to nervous in less than a minute. Before I can ask what's wrong, I hear it.

Shouting.

"Are we," she pauses, whispering while wringing her hands. I put up my hand and shake my head. I can't make out much beyond someone is shouting, and her talking is now suddenly a risk.

My heart thundering in my chest, I approach the door slowly, straining to hear what's happening beyond the door. I can feel a bead of sweat gather at my temple before it slowly starts to run down my face. It takes everything in me not to show my fear in front of my patient, who is beginning to hyperventilate.

With my ear pressed to the door, I close my eyes, trying to block everything out except what might be happening out there. At first, the shouting remains indistinct. And then, probably within seconds, it clarifies into more distinct sounds: many people shouting, and the surprisingly loud clicks of camera shutters. My eyes snap open when I realize what I'm hearing.

Shit.

"Mackenzie? We're alright. I know it sounds scary outside, but it's nothing to be worried about." I step up to her on the table and gently squeeze her shoulder. She's shaking now, looking at me, her face stricken. There's no doubt in my mind she's been in an active shooter situation in the past, and the shouting from down the hall has triggered her.

Despite my fury at what is no doubt happening outside, I coach Mackenzie through her anxiety attack. It takes several minutes, but eventually she comes back to her body and understands that she's safe. I force myself to walk her through her injury and connect her with our Ortho department. By the time we're done, she's back to being upset about her teammate stomping on her foot and taking her out of the game for the next few weeks.

When I finally step out, the end of the hallway is quiet. Security must have cleared the paparazzi out finally. As I walk toward the nurses' station, I allow myself a moment to believe that they weren't here because of me. That some high-profile celebrity is here, and that's why they swarmed our ER floor for the better part of an hour. But when I make eye contact with our charge nurse, I see the truth in her eyes.

They were here for me.

***

"Dr. Masters," Dr. Jordan, the lead attending for the entire ER Department, stares me down from the other side of her desk. I do my best not to fidget under her scrutiny. Next to my dad, she's the practitioner I look up to the most. She has an eagle eye for detail, and won't hesitate to ream you for missing things. She's a dragon and I am lucky to learn from her.

Today might be the first time I don't feel so lucky.

"I'm not going to pretend like what occurred today wasn't a complete and utter disaster. Nor will I sugarcoat what I have to say next."

This is it. My career is over. I let myself have a boyfriend, and now I've flushed ten years of training and dedication down the drain... What will my dad think?

"While we were able to get them off our property and hopefully scare them enough with the threat of lawsuits for blocking the ambulance bay, knowing who you are currently *dating*, they'll likely be back." She says dating with such disdain, I'd be surprised she ever felt romantic attachment if I didn't already know she has a life partner.

"And if this becomes a frequent problem, the hospital may have to re-evaluate our staffing." She lets it hang there, the vague threat. If I can't get the paparazzi to leave me alone at work, I'll lose my job. And any hope I have of achieving my career goals.

"I understand." I get up, knowing I'm dismissed once she starts typing on her keyboard. "It won't happen again."

As I slip out the door, she speaks again, filling me with dread.

"I hope he's worth it."

I hate that I don't have an answer.

***

Beauford: Hey bestie, I'm in another bind tonight. Any chance you can take my shift? Word on the street is you could use some kudos points with Dr. J after the drama earlier this week.

I stare at Beauford's text, simultaneously wishing I could slap him, while also acknowledging how right he is. After the paparazzi debacle, I'm desperate to get back into Dr. Jordan's good graces. And if I don't do it soon, I may never recover, even without another visit from the paps.

As I pick up my phone to reply, my eye catches on the dress I'm supposed to be wearing tonight. Jason's newest movie, a political thriller, is premiering tonight, and I promised to meet him there.

Before I let myself think too much, I fire off a couple of texts and throw my scrubs back on. I just have to hope he'll understand.

CHAPTER 20

JASON

Where is she? I try not to pace as I stand near the theater entrance, waiting for Alexis. My parents and sister are already inside, along with my castmates and most of the other premier guests. I shake out my hands and tug on my suddenly tight collar. Even after decades of acting, premier night always puts me on edge.

My phone dings and I nearly shout with relief. She obviously got caught up in traffic and will be here shortly. I didn't love that we had to arrive separately, but we were coming from different ends of L.A. and would have been dumb to try to come together.

But when I read her message, my heart sinks to my shoes. My eyes start to feel hot and itchy, and I quickly realize it's because I'm about to cry. Fuck, this hurts.

> **Alexis:** I'm so sorry, Jason, I got called in. I know tonight is going to be amazing. I wish I could be there.

"You could be," I whisper at the screen, using the heel of my palm to wipe away the tears that've managed to fall. "You're choosing not to."

In a daze, I reply, then head into the theater, no longer nervous about the premier. Instead, all I feel is disappointment.

***

I'm exhausted as I step off the elevator and start to head down the hall. The cast and crew afterparty lasted well into the early morning, and when I normally would have bowed out, I stayed, trying to drown my frustration in alcohol and friends. Which I mostly regret since I now smell like a college bar and still feel just as shitty.

I do my best not to look at her door as I pass by, but fail completely. And instead of finding my bed, I find myself staring at Alexis. She must have been watching for me to pass by. She looks tired and distressed, her brow pinched, shadows under her eyes, and a suspicious shine in them. Seeing these clear signs of pain is a blow to the gut, and I silently follow her inside when I meant to spend a rare night alone in my apartment.

"Alexis, I'm beat. I just want to go to bed." I scrub my hands over my face, trying to dispel some of my anxiety. We stand an awkward distance from each other in her living room. Alexis' arms are around her abdomen, like she's holding herself together.

"I'm tired too, Jason," her voice is raw, catching as she says my name. "But we need to talk about this. I don't want to go to bed until we do."

It's the quiet plea in her voice that makes me cave.

"Alright, you want to do this right now? Then fine." My voice comes out wrong, angry sounding. She flinches, but lifts her chin, as if preparing herself for battle. But that's not what I want. That's never what I want.

"Alexis, you left me hanging tonight." My voice cracks as the pain I felt earlier tonight rushes back, settling heavily in my chest.

"I know, I'm sorry." She presses her lips together, blinking rapidly. "I just... I feel so much pressure right now, with work. And with the paparazzi fiasco, I needed to prove that I'm all in, that I'm not letting you distract me."

I feel like she just slapped me. Distract her? Is that how she sees our relationship?

"So, what, because I'm not out saving people, my work isn't worthy of your support?" I don't bother trying to hide how hurt I am. I may not love my job, or how it makes me a public figure, but I'm still proud of my films, and I want her to be proud of me too.

"No!" She steps forward, reaching for me, but pulls short. Like she isn't sure of what to do or say. "That's not what I meant." She rubs her forehead, eyes wide and distressed.

"I just mean that, as my residency winds down, I have to be all-in, especially if I want any chance of getting hired as an attending. This is the nature of my job; this is going to happen more often than you want. There are going to be times when I have to be a doctor first, and a girlfriend second. Can you understand that?"

I want to say no, but the truth is I do understand. The pressure on medical professionals is incredibly high, especially as the pandemic continues to put a strain on the system. And as an ER doctor, she's often making life and death decisions for her patients.

Instead of fighting more, and risking everything, I close the distance between us and pull her into my arms. Holding tight. The ugly feeling in my chest easing as her head rests on my shoulder. Exactly where it belongs.

CHAPTER 21

ALEXIS

"You're right, I'm sorry. Let's just go to bed."

At first, my sleep deprived brain doesn't really register what he's saying, it's just happy to be in his arms again. But once the words sink in, I pull back.

"Jason, no. Don't do that. Don't just give in and set your feelings aside like that." My hands slide up to his cheeks, forcing him to look me in the eye. His blue eyes look so sad. Because of me and my choices. And that guts me inside.

He closes them and gently pulls my hands away shaking his head. "Lex, I'm just tired, so are you. There's no point in arguing about this further when you're right. This is going to happen, probably more often than not for the next few years. I just need to get used to it. It's ok."

Frustration boils up, getting caught in my throat. Because it's not ok for him to feel like his life, his work doesn't matter as much. Or that he just needs to take this disappointment and not feel upset about it. Instead of fighting for his own needs, he's letting them go in favor of keeping the peace. If I've learned anything in therapy, it's that keeping our emotions bottled leads nowhere.

He leaves me and heads to my bedroom. Despite my frustration, I can't help but feel some relief that he isn't trying to leave. I follow, ready to keep fighting. But when I find him in my bathroom, brushing his teeth, leaning against the wall with his eyes closed, all the fight leaves me. It's clear talking more will do nothing but make things worse.

We're silent as we prepare for bed. And when we climb in, he doesn't pull me to him like he normally does. Instead, he lays with his back to me, seemingly asleep the moment his head hits the pillow.

I lie awake for longer than I should, tormented by what that might mean. It's not until early morning light begins to filter in that he rolls over, pulling me into his body. I don't hesitate to wrap my arms around him tightly, pressing our bodies so close that we might as well be fused. Tears of relief soak my cheeks and his shirt.

"Shhhh…" His big hand combs through my hair then down my back, "We're ok, I promise. Get some sleep." Eventually, I fall asleep to the rhythm of his heartbeat and the feel of his lips in my hair.

***

Alexis: Emergency girls' day required. I think everyone's off today, right?

Allison: Yes, but you'll have to come here. It's my weekend with the kids.

Tristan: I'll get donuts, everything ok?

Alexis: Yes? No?

Alexis: Honestly, I don't know how I feel. I just need my girls right now.

Kiki: We ride at dawn. I'll bring the wine. And maybe a nutcracker?

***

"Ok, the kids are in the basement with their movie bribe. They won't come upstairs unless they need more popcorn. Spill."

We're gathered in Allison's cozy living room, Tristan and Allison sharing the couch, while I occupy the armchair, clutching a pillow like it's a life vest. Nique is seated on the floor, ominously cracking walnuts. Apparently, she wasn't just making a joke when she suggested bringing a nutcracker. I cringe as she joyfully cracks another. I really hope she isn't imagining someone specific while she does that.

Taking a deep breath, I explain what happened. Starting with the paparazzi, Dr. Jordan's comments, me picking up a shift, and our fight. If you could even call it that.

"I think I'm more upset by how quickly he just gave in? I never want him to think that he can't have feelings about something, even if they're directed at me or something I've done. How could that bode well for our future if he's constantly stifling himself?"

All three sit back, quiet at first. Allison, probably unsurprisingly given her current marital status, chimes in first.

"Sweetie, you know I love you, right?" I nod. Allison has her mom voice on, which means I'm about to receive a bit of tough love. "Your job will ruin your relationship if you and Jason don't sit down and establish some rules of conduct." I open my mouth to argue, but she just puts her hand up, clearly not done.

"Phil and I are struggling right now because we didn't do that and he let his work consume him to the point where I no longer had a husband and partner, but someone who occasionally slept in our bed and paid our bills. You need guardrails. A clear understanding of when, where, and how your job takes precedence over personal things. You two need to establish when it's ok to skip something in favor of work, and when it's not. The caveat being things that are life threatening, of course. But if you don't have this conversation, you two will keep finding yourselves in this situation, and it might eventually break you."

I nod, trying to absorb what she's saying. She's probably right, she and her husband have been in counseling for nearly a year now. This is probably something they learned in therapy.

"Allison's right, you two need to be clear on what's important to you both. You're so used to only being beholden to yourself that it will probably take some trial and error to learn how to navigate things as a couple. But you'll get there. And you'll always have us to lean on." Tristian reaches across and squeezes my hand. Her reassurance is a balm to my frayed heart. I love these women more than I can truly express.

"And if you can't figure it out, I've got the perfect nutcracker to use. For intimidation purposes only, of course." Kiki waves the heavy metal instrument around, winking, causing us all to laugh and groan at the same time. She's definitely a ballbuster, and that'll probably never change.

"Thanks, I feel better now. And you're right, Jason and I need to talk about it in depth." I take a healthy gulp of wine and turn toward Allison. "Now that we've solved all my problems, what about you and Phil? You're coming to the end of the year you set. Any changes?"

Allison sighs and takes her own large sip. "Yes and no. In many ways, Phil has done everything I've asked. Shown me that he's committed to healing our marriage and not letting his work get in the way again. But part of me isn't ready to trust him. I'm feeling a little lost."

"What has your marriage counselor said about it?" Tristan reaches over and takes her free hand, squeezing it like she did for me.

"Well, she's encouraged me to let him back home. To trust him again. Because technically, he's done everything that I've asked of him, and more. She says it's unfair to not give him the chance to keep proving himself."

"You know I'm the last person to jump to a man's defense, but I've seen how amazing you and Phil are together, and I think your therapist is right. It's time to let yourself be happy again." We all turn and stare at Kiki like she's suddenly grown two heads. "What? I can be nice to men when I want to. And if anyone with a penis deserves a second chance, it's Phil. I mean come on, guys.... It's *Phil*."

We all nod because she's not wrong. Phil is one of those guys who draws everyone into his sphere and makes them feel seen and welcome. When we first heard of their marriage troubles over a year ago, we were all shocked. I can't describe the relief I feel for my friend that she and her husband seem to be making things work. If they can do it, so can Jason and I.

CHAPTER 22

JASON

The last twenty-four hours have been hell. So, when a hand suddenly claps my shoulder from behind, I nearly jump out of my skin. I have no idea how long I've been standing at the Craft Services table for. "Dude, jumpy much? You know you can have a donut. We're not kids anymore, there's no one on set who can chastise us for eating some sugar."

I turn to find Eddie, a longtime friend and colleague, standing next to me, eyeing the donuts. Despite my shitty mood, I smile, exchanging a back slapping hug with him, "Hey, man. What're you doing on set?" Eddie had left the *Agent Smith* franchise a couple films ago, so it's been a while since he's been on set.

"Didn't you hear? They're having Olena and I film a flashback scene. Apparently, the footage they already had didn't quite fit the emotions they were looking to evoke for her final fight." He shrugs, snagging a chocolate glazed donut and fitting the whole thing in his mouth. "It happened to fit into my schedule, so I don't mind coming in and getting some extra cash. How's filming going in general? Are you ready to say goodbye to *Agent Smith*?"

As he's talking, a vague memory comes to the surface about adding some flashback scenes. Everyone wants to go out with a bang with this final installment. As for me? I'm just ready to set this franchise aside and move on. After nearly ten years, it's time.

"Mostly ready. It's definitely time to move on. I'm just not sure what's next."

He nods, probably familiar with the feeling after leaving the franchise himself. After so many years working on the same story, with the same cast, and mostly the same crew, it's hard to transition to new projects. "It was definitely weird at first, but you get used to it. Any ideas for what's next?"

I open my mouth to give my canned response but stop. Eddie and I have been buddies for years, decades, if there's anyone I should be willing to open up to, it's him. Alexis' encouragement a few weeks ago pushes me to blurt out, "I've been thinking about taking a break from acting and doing some writing."

Eddie blinks, a stunned expression on his face. "You serious?"

"Yeah," I shrug, heart pounding.

"Well, you're certainly rich enough to afford it. But man, do you realize how hard it is to make it in publishing? Most authors barely cover their costs, let alone make a profit. Not to mention the public scrutiny you'd get. Not sure it'd be worth it, if I'm being honest." His hand comes back to my shoulder, probably trying to seem reassuring, but it just feels condescending. But he's just confirmed what I've always feared, that even my closest friends don't see much value in me switching careers.

Fuck, that stings.

"You're probably right. It's just one of those crazy things that I've always thought would be fun to try. I'm probably just thinking about it more because I haven't picked my next project. Once I do, things will go back to normal."

"You'll be fine, I promise. Now tell me all about this doctor you're dating, I've been dying to hear all the details."

***

When I get home that night, I'm exhausted, frustrated, and embarrassed. All I want to do is sink into Alexis and forget that today even happened.

So, when she walks out of her room to greet me, I waste no time hauling her up and locking our lips together. She doesn't hesitate to return my kiss, eagerly wrapping her legs around my waist and opening to me. I pull back just for a moment, "I know we need to talk, and we will, but right now I just need you."

"Ok," she whispers, pulling my lips back down to hers as we tumble onto the bed. Despite everything being shit, I know I'm right where I'm meant to be.

Chapter 23

Alexis

"Don't you dare laugh."

"Alexis!" Jason gasps, his face turning red as he tries not to laugh. "What you're asking is impossible. I'm sorry." He then proceeds to fall apart he's laughing so hard.

Why is Jason laughing? Great question.

My devil cat decided it would be a smart idea to parkour around the apartment this morning while Jason and I slept. And somehow, her tiny lil' nine-pound body managed to connect with my bookshelf with enough force to send it crashing to the floor. The sound was so loud that it jump scared me awake so hard I fell out of bed and peed myself a bit out of fear and confusion.

And Jason? What did he do? That motherfucker slept through the whole thing.

How? No idea. But he sure as shit woke up when I smacked him in the face with a pillow five times.

And now he's laughing at the carnage.

"This isn't funny!"

"I'm sorry, babe, but it is. Slinky is *tiny*, and how she managed this is beyond me. And you?"

"Don't you fucking say a thing about me." I glare at him hard, opening my eyes wide in what my family affectionately calls my crazy eyes, so he knows I mean business. We may not have been dating for long, but Jason knows what this look means.

"Woah, woah, woah, ok. It's no longer funny." His hands land on my shoulders, rubbing the tension knots that are permanently there. "Tell you what, you hop in the shower, and I'll get started on cleaning this up. Then we can go to the store later and buy you a new shelf."

Yes, because not only did my cat somehow knock over the bookshelf, it landed on my couch in a way that completely demolished the structure. There's no saving it. At least I didn't have any breakable things on it, only books.

I nod and shuffle to the bathroom, simultaneously furious with Slinky and incredibly relieved she didn't kill herself. I spend a lot of time just standing under the hot water, trying to get it to erase the fact that I actually peed myself in fear.

To be fair, it wasn't like I released my whole bladder or anything. But it's still humiliating.

Much, much later, I step out of the bathroom to find the bookshelf is gone, wood chips cleared, and my books are stacked neatly against the wall. The apartment is quiet, so Jason must have stepped out to get coffee; a quick glance at his spot on my key holder confirms it. A few days ago, we exchanged keys for easy access and safety. It was weirdly serious and emotional? Like the keys symbolized how deeply we felt and cared somehow? It was weird and wonderful.

I'm fully dressed and feel less hateful toward my cat when Jason returns with coffee and pastries. Before forcing ourselves to the store, we do our normal morning routine on my balcony. We're at the point in our relationship where either of us could get recognized in public, so we both wear ball caps and sunglasses whenever we do shit like this.

It would be exhausting if Jason didn't make it fun.

"Ok, today, we're Mr. and Mrs. Smith, and we're on a mission to find an evil mafia lord hell-bent on blowing up the Hollywood sign."

Every time we go out like this, he comes up with a prompt, and we have to act our way through the store or event following the prompt. Last time we were secret lovers from Regency England, and we couldn't touch openly in public. I also pretended to faint a few times so that Jason had to catch me. We always end up spending more time acting out scenes than we do the actual task we're out in public to do. But it takes the pressure off being out and being seen and makes me laugh.

The added bonus is that almost every candid photo of us out there is us laughing or having fun. They're the type of photos that show how much we love and respect each other. I even used one for my phone background. Which is a bit ridiculous.

So today, we're spies. Slowly moving up and down the furniture store aisles. Peeking around corners, trying to find our enemy before they find us.

We get the odd look here and there, but mostly, we fly under the radar. And most importantly, we have fun, and this morning's shock begins to fade away.

A few hours and a lunch break later, we're back at my apartment. The box containing the new shelving unit staring at me from the floor. Jason had to take a call and went back to his own apartment. Something to do with the release schedule and press for his upcoming movie.

So, here I am, alone, eyeing the box like it's an uncrackable safe instead of cardboard.

"Alright, Alexis, you can do this. Your boyfriend very nicely cleaned everything up, went with you to pick out a bigger and better bookcase, *and* helped you get it inside. You are a smart woman. You went to med school, and you're almost done with residency. You can open this box, follow the directions, and build this damn thing all by yourself."

Slinky takes this exact moment to yowl at me loudly from the couch, clearly saying *Ha! Yeah, good luck with that*. She has no faith in me, clearly.

Using a pair of kitchen scissors, I slice open the box and start yanking things out. All the while chanting in my head: *I can do this, I can do this, I can do this.*

***

"I CAN'T DO THIS!"

I've flopped on the ground, pieces strewn everywhere, the directions packet tossed across the room. Nothing makes sense, and I feel like an idiot. Tears of shame are leaking out of my eyes, and I can't even be bothered to wipe them away.

Jason chooses this moment to walk in.

He stands there momentarily, observing me in the middle of the chaos, tipping his head to one side.

"This must not be going well, hunh?" He says it so neutrally, without a drop of judgment or humor, like it's no big deal that I can't figure this out. Which, of course, sets off a wave of tears.

He gets down on the floor with me and helps me sit up. While wiping my tears, he kisses my brow. All at once, tension leaves my body. I may not know how to build pre-fab furniture, but I have a partner who will help me. Always.

"Why don't you get started on dinner, and I'll tackle this. Sound good?" I nod mutely, pulling him in for a quick peck before getting up and starting dinner. While I cook, he builds. By the time I have the table set, the bookcase is up and ready for my books. Why is he so wonderful?

"Jason, food's ready. Let's eat and then put my books away after. Maybe we should watch *Princess Bride* in the background?"

"Perfect idea." He sits next to me at the table and rubs his hands together at the sight of the spaghetti and meatballs I made. It's nothing fancy. I didn't have much energy to do anything too crazy, but with the amount of garlic I add to the pasta sauce, it's fucking good.

We leave the dishes for tomorrow and spend our evening watching *our* movie and methodically reorganizing my books. There's nothing wildly different about tonight; we've done similar things together plenty of times. But for some reason, it feels like something shifted tonight. In a way that's irreversible. And it doesn't scare me.

CHAPTER 24

JASON

"Oooooh, yes." Alexis moans.

"Yes, Jason! Right there. Holy shit. Don't stop. That's the spot."

My dick twitches in my pants, and I can feel it getting hard. I've been reciting what I can remember of the periodic table, trying to keep myself from getting aroused. It's not working.

Alexis is lying on her stomach on the bed, and I am dutifully trying to massage out some knots she has. I'm trying to be a good boyfriend who cares for the woman he loves, not just uses her to get his dick wet.

But she's making it really hard.

No pun intended.

"Alexis? Babe, you have got to stop making sex noises. My poor dick doesn't understand that this is a friendly, non-sexy back rub."

She giggles, "But Jason, your hands are magic! What else am I supposed to do?" She giggles again, then pinches her lips together. And for about a minute, I think she's got herself under control. Nope. Spoke too soon.

"Oooooooooooooh, that's it. Yes, yes, yes, yes, yes!"

Fuck me.

Not willing to torture myself any longer, I flip her over, ready to tickle her until she regrets making all that noise. But when I finally get her facing me, the heat in her eyes changes my mind.

"Finally, Jason, it took you forever to break and give in. You held out, buddy." She cracks a huge smile, and I find myself smiling back. The little shit.

Instead of tickling the crap out of her, I lean over her and kiss her slowly. As soon as she starts to pant and squirm, I pull back, giving her my most innocent smile. "I gotta shower and get ready for filming. I'll see you later." I give her one more quick kiss before getting up, ignoring her squawk of protest.

"Seriously? You suck!"

I chuckle and internally apologize to my dick, who is currently weeping. "Two can play at this game, Alexis! You messed with the master. I love you, and I'll see you later."

As quickly as I can, I exit her apartment and head to mine. I really need to head out and get on set for filming.

***

Hours later, I'm in my trailer eating an apple quick when my phone dings.

> **Alexis:** Hope you're having a good time on set. Don't think I've forgiven you for earlier…. I'm only texting you because I thought you should know we've apparently secretly gotten married. [article link attached]

I click the link with a sigh. Great, wonder what they decided to misconstrue this time?

ARE JASON ADAMS AND ALEXIS MASTERS SECRETLY MARRIED?
LOOKS LIKE WEDDED BLISS TO US

The article is peppered with pictures of us picking up her bookcase and hauling it to her car. They even have a shot of us goofing off in the bathroom section of the store. We look deliriously happy, so I can see why they want to use these to say we're married.

> **Jason:** For fuck's sake. I think we should just ignore this one. If we see more articles come out saying the same thing, we can make a statement, but for now let's see if this one just dies on its own.

Jason: Miss your hot bod already. Be ready for some good fucking when I get home.

Alexis: [contemplating GIF]

Alexis: Hmmmmmmmmmmmmm. I'm not sure my tease of a boyfriend deserves access to this pussy after the stunt he pulled. I might just use my vibe and leave it at that.

Jason: [Puss in Boots begging GIF]

Jason: Aw, babe, please don't do that. My poor dick will be so sad!

Alexis: [Louise cackling GIF]

Alexis: I guess you'll just have to hope I'm in a better mood when you get home.

Jason: Shit, they're ready for us to get back to it. Do not, I repeat, do not take care of yourself. I've got you, babe.

Before leaving my trailer, I quickly submit Alexis' favorite late-night snack order and arrange for it to be delivered. Hopefully, this will get me in her good graces. Fuck, I need to get today wrapped soon. My girl needs me.

***

Alexis: I'm waiting..... [picture attached]

I nearly spit out the water I'm chugging when I see the photo Alexis sent me a couple of hours ago. She's on our bed, wearing a lacy body suit of some kind. She posed so that the light shines behind her, illuminating her shape without showing everything. It's so damn sexy I get hard just looking at it. I need to get home *now*.

When I step through the bedroom door, though, she's fast asleep. She looks so peaceful. I don't even consider waking her up; I just move about the apartment, shutting things down before crawling into bed next to her and pulling her close. She makes a few soft sleep noises before settling into my arms. My heart squeezes in my chest; this woman is everything to me, and I'm starting to think that forever with her will never be enough.

Chapter 25

Alexis

The next few weeks pass by quickly. Full of sex, I love you's, and attempts at dates where the paparazzi don't find us. We're winning at about 60/40 with them at the moment.

Tonight, though, we're going to a party.

After a string of shootings, two with police officers involved, I'm ready for some time when I can turn my brain off. The whole hospital has been on edge. Shootings are traumatic enough for staff to treat, but add in officer-involved shootings where it's unclear if the violence was justified, and the hospital becomes a powder keg of differing opinions. Most of us know that police violence against people of color is disproportionate, but there's always one or two staff who still staunchly believe the police are always justified. This can lead to horrible tension and, on some occasions, shouting matches in breakrooms or hallways. I even had to send two male nurses to opposite sides of the hospital this week because they were about to throw punches in the middle of the cafeteria.

So yeah, this week has been incredibly difficult.

The party tonight is black and white themed. When I asked Jason why the hell this sounded like a party out of high school or college, he shrugged and said, "Mitch is kind of immature. He only throws themed parties, but his house in Malibu is amazing, and it's almost always a blast. So, people put up with it. We'll have fun, I promise."

This will be my first official "Hollywood" party, so I'm a little nervous. But with the theme, I feel like I can pull something together with what I have in my closet and not feel out of place. Jason said, and I quote, "I'll want to rip off anything you wear anyway, so buying anything new would be pointless." Honestly, his caveman side is off the charts sometimes.

At least the media frenzy over us has died down. We actually have Jason's ex to thank for that, sadly enough. She disappeared shortly after their very public breakup. She'd been caught in public more than once with other men, and when Jason confronted her, it dissolved into a shouting match on the sidewalk. A few days ago, it was leaked that she was currently at a recovery center for alcohol abuse. Jason and I had a long talk when the news broke. He felt so guilty for not seeing how much she was struggling and failing to help her. I only did a few rotations in psych during med school, so I couldn't give him much insight beyond that it wasn't his fault. Sure, he could have pushed harder when it was clear she was unhappy, but ultimately, people need to be ready to receive help for it to have a lasting effect. I can tell that didn't completely assuage his guilt, though, and every once in a while, I've caught him staring off at something, and I know he's running through their relationship, trying to pick apart every sign he missed.

I suggested he see a therapist, which made him defensive. We talked about my therapy journey and how much it has helped me cope with my job and the demands of being a medical professional frequently dealing with life and death situations. It wasn't an easy conversation, but he came down from "absolutely not" to "I'll think about it." Which is all I can ask for, really.

But for now, I'm headed to my favorite brunch place to see my girls.

"DETAILS! I need details now." Nique is holding my hand from across the table, staring daggers straight into my eyes. Even though I've seen all three of them often at work, I've shared very little. Mostly because I don't love personal talk in the workplace, but also because I was still enjoying the honeymoon phase of our relationship.

"I know what kind of details you want, Kiki, but I will not be sharing those. I *will* say, though, that I am *never* unsatisfied." I pause for dramatic effect, "and neither is he!" I wink, causing all three to dissolve into hooting and exaggerated fainting. God, these girls are the best.

"Ok, ok, ok!" Allison throws her arms out, trying to regain control. "Kiki asked the wrong question. The *real* question is: have you both said the L-word yet? Because those photos from that charity auction and that date you guys had last week? Woowee, the L-word was practically *pouring* out of your eyes!" She smiles at me, hopefully bouncing in her seat. Of the three of my friends, she is the most romantic. You would think that after separating from her husband last year, she would be disillusioned by romantic love. But if you ask her, she'll maintain that love is always possible if you're willing to be open to it.

I bite my lip, trying not to smile too hard. I feel like all I do lately is smile when I think about Jason.

"Not that it is truly any of your business, but yes, we're serious and saying 'I love you.'" We all sigh collectively.

"Oh, Lex, we're so happy for you! When can we hang out with him again as a group? I feel like last time, it just dissolved into an interrogation. Now that you're official, we should get to know him as friends." Tristan nudges me with her shoulder just as the server reaches our table with our food.

We're silent for the next few minutes, filling our faces with the best brunch in our neighborhood. Hell, maybe even in the city.

Once we've eaten at least half of our food, I follow up on Tristan's request. "He would love to have a group hang with you three, he keeps asking, actually. He leaves tomorrow for two weeks of filming on location before they wrap. He gets home the day before my parents descend, so we will both need a break from them at some point." All three snicker; they know my mom well and know exactly how much she'll drive me up the wall.

"But, enough about me. I want to hear what you three have been up to lately. I feel like we haven't had enough time to talk recently, and when we do, it's always about Jason and me."

By the time we head out to go about our days, the serving staff is practically shoving us out.

***

A few hours later, Jason and I are in his car, headed to the party. He has one hand on the wheel, and the other holds my hand. I love that he just adopted my quiet time routine without question. I even think he likes it a bit.

Tonight, he's dressed in dark wash jeans; they aren't quite black, but they work, and a black dress shirt. I'm in a pair of white jeans and a silky cream tank. I have a black bralette on too that made Jason's eyes nearly fall out of his head. His obsession with my boobs is almost comical at this point.

When we finally enter the party, and I have a chance to see the guests, I let go of the rest of my anxiety over my outfit. Jason was right, people are dressed nicely but on theme, and in nothing that screams, "I paid a thousand dollars for these jeans." When he sees me scanning the crowd, he pulls me in close and pops a kiss against my temple. "See, babe? I told you; you'd be the hottest one here tonight." I just roll my eyes. I don't know about that, but I know that it's true, at least in Jason's eyes.

We meet Mitch and a litany of other guests. Jason was right; Mitch is immature, but in the class clown kind of way that makes him endearing. I don't think I've seen him sit down once, moving through the crowd constantly, checking in, and catching up. Nearly two hours in, and I feel like I've met everyone I've ever wanted to meet in Hollywood. A few times, Jason has had to pinch me to snap me out of my awe. It would be embarrassing if anyone were anything but friendly and gracious about it.

I'm stuffing a mini crab cake into my mouth when I feel *it*. The familiar gush that every menstruating person knows. Blood completely drains from my face, and I nearly choke on the food I'm swallowing.

No, no, no, no, no!

My hand latches onto Jason's forearm, tugging urgently. He looks down and then does a double-take once he sees my expression. "Babe, what's wrong? Is the crab no good?"

I shake my head vigorously, trying to school my features, so no one else notices my distress. "Bathroom! I need the bathroom. Where is it?" I'm starting to stress sweat.

"It's just down the hall there, first door on the right." I'm off before he even finishes his sentence. Please, please, please let there be no one in there.

I nearly kiss the person who exits just as I reach the door, and once I'm in, I quickly lock it, kick out of my shoes and yank down my jeans. No wonder they felt a little tighter than expected when I wiggled into them earlier tonight.

The period gods must be feeling benevolent tonight because there's only a tiny drop of blood on the crotch of my jeans; I bet you can't even see it from the other side. My underwear, however? Absolute massacre in there.

The first day of my cycle is always a gusher, then it tapers off and is pretty chill for the next four. I track my period on my calendar, and it's supposed to start in a few days. I guess the stress from work lately made Aunt Flo visit me a little early. And *of course,* it had to be at a Black and White themed party in which I chose to wear all white! Fuck me.

I whip off the underwear and toss them in the sink. I then take a huge length of toilet paper and fold it several times, making a makeshift pad and stuffing it between my legs. I then spend the next several minutes riffling through every drawer and cabinet, looking for *anything* I can use. When I can't find any period products of any variety, I turn to my underwear, trying to rinse out all the blood. Maybe I can get them clean and dry enough for the trip home?

There's a knock at the door that startles me, and I realize I've been in here a long time. "Occupied!" Fuck, I don't want anyone one to know! I'm a grown-ass adult, I shouldn't be surprised by my own period anymore!

"Alexis, it's Jason. You ok in there? Are you sick?" He sounds worried, and oddly, it calms me a bit. I'm reminded that I'm not here alone; there's a man outside who loves me and will do anything to help me right now. I unlock the door, open it just enough for him to enter, and then lock it again.

When I turn, he's staring at me in shock. I almost laugh.

"Uh, babe. Why aren't you wearing pants or underwear? Better yet, why does it look like you murdered someone in the sink?"

Now I do laugh. Because from his perspective, this is pretty perplexing. He looks so cute when he's confused.

"Well, Hollywood. This is what happens when your period makes a surprise appearance a few days early."

"Oh shit, ok. What can I do to help?" I could kiss him right now. Of course, his first thought is to ask how he can help, not be grossed out. He's so wonderful. Too wonderful, honestly, because now I'm crying.

His worry turns into alarm as he sees the tears slip out. "Oh no! Honey, don't cry. I'm right here to help; just tell me what you need." He pulls me into his arms, rubbing his hands up and down my back, lips pressed to my temple.

I give myself a minute in his arms before I pull myself together and take a step back. "Jason, I need you to find the kindest, chillest, least likely to gossip woman out there and ask if they have a tampon or pad. And then we are going to head home so I can wallow in ice cream."

He's nodding vigorously, heading for the door. Before he can open it, I add, "And tell Mitch that he is a nearly forty-year-old man. The least he can do is provide a few period products in his guest bathroom for when he hosts parties." Jason shoots me a thumbs up, then slips out the door, careful to keep anyone who might be in the hall from seeing me.

He returns only minutes later with a tampon, and I take care of business. Once I feel sufficiently put back together, we exit the bathroom and leave. Jason said he'd call Mitch tomorrow and let him know we had fun, but needed to leave. And pass along the period product advice.

I'm staring sullenly out the window as we drive home, so I don't immediately notice that we've pulled off the freeway until the car stops. We're at a convenience store. Before I can ask Jason why we're here, he asks, "What kind of ice cream do you want? I know most women like chocolate too, anything in particular you like? Or snacks? Are you low on your own period products? I think they might sell some here."

Before I can stop myself, I burst into tears. Again. He doesn't question my reaction, just takes my hand in his and rubs the back of it, waiting me out. Just when I didn't think I could love him anymore, the feeling grows a little deeper.

It takes a minute, but I calm down enough to make my ice cream and candy request. "Oh, and bacon, if they have some that looks ok, grab some." He doesn't even question it, just adds it to the list he started on his phone before heading in.

Twenty minutes later, we are back at my apartment.

"Lex, why don't you hop in the shower? I'll grab you some clean underwear and PJs and get started on the bacon." He gives my ass a light slap and sends me toward the bathroom while making a beeline for the kitchen himself.

I laugh when I step out of the steamy shower a while later. On the counter is my largest pair of grannie panties and my unicorn onesie. This man *knows* me.

After a snack of bacon and rocky road ice cream, we're snuggled into bed, just holding each other.

"Hey, can I ask you something?"

"Go for it, Doc. You know you can ask me anything."

"If you could do anything besides being an actor, what would you be?"

Chapter 26

Jason

I can't stop myself from tensing up when she asks. Even though I knew she would eventually want to ask me these kinds of questions, I'm not ready.

I've never shared this with anyone, and even though I love her and know she'd be nothing but encouraging, my insecurities rear their ugly heads.

She waits patiently, not pushing for my answer, just running her hand up and down my forearm.

I take a deep breath, gathering my courage, and tell her.

"I'd be a writer." I pause, waiting to see if she laughs or reacts negatively. When she remains silent, I push on. "I've always loved writing, and my English teachers growing up always encouraged me. They said I was good, and one even urged me to enter a writing contest. But I don't know. By then I knew acting was what my parents expected me to do, so I just never pursued it." I shrug, trying to sound casual about it. Like it doesn't bother me.

"And now? How do you feel about writing now?"

I should have known she wouldn't let it go. Alexis knew she wanted to be a doctor at a young age and made it happen. For her, pursuing your passion is the most important thing a person can do. And I don't disagree, I just feel like some passions aren't meant to be.

"I've written a few short stories and tried longer-form works. But I'm so busy acting and traveling that I never finish most of them. It doesn't really matter; it was just a childhood dream."

She sits up, turning to face me. She has the cute little furrow in her brow she gets when she's frustrated, but trying not to show it.

"But, Jason. You're thirty-one now. You've had an incredibly successful acting career, and I know your parents are proud of you. Don't you think it's time for you to at least try? You said it yourself, you aren't feeling very inspired by the projects you've been offered. Maybe it's a sign that you need to try this?"

It takes all of my self-control not to roll my eyes and scoff. I know she is coming from a place of love and support, but she doesn't understand. Acting is all I'm good for.

"Lex, thank you, but no. I'm just in a bit of a slump right now. The right project will come along, and I'll be fine."

"But."

"Alexis, I'm sorry. I know you just want to help and be supportive, but I really don't want to keep discussing this. Please drop it." I feel like an ass, but I'm starting to feel clammy and anxious. If she keeps pushing, I might say something I don't mean, and I don't want to hurt her.

Every time I think about leaving acting and trying something new, the old feelings of inadequacy start to creep in. Growing up, I knew my parents loved us, but it was a distant kind of love. They were traveling constantly, leaving us at home more often than not so we could be in school. It wasn't until I started acting that it felt like my parents saw me. They became so invested, so quickly, that before I even realized it, my career was taking off and the idea of doing something different felt impossible. I finally had the attention that I craved from my parents, giving that up was out of the question. Now that I'm in my thirties, making a major shift seems even more out of reach than ever before. And talking about it now will lead nowhere.

She sits there for a moment, studying my face. I can tell she doesn't want to stop talking but seems to decide to drop it. At least for now.

She lays back down, letting me pull her close again. I can feel her body start to grow heavy as she relaxes. I know she's about to fall asleep.

"I hope you'll trust me enough someday to let me read your work." She sighs sleepily, nuzzling deeper under the covers. "I just know you're amazing at it."

I don't say anything back; my emotions are stuck in my throat. How does she always manage to disarm me completely? For maybe the first time since I was in school, I actually want someone to read my work. The thought is terrifying.

***

It's very early when I force myself to leave her bed. Shooting starts later this morning, but it's a long drive, and I need to get out on the road soon if I want to make it in time. I look down at Alexis, who has pulled my pillow into her arms and is clutching it tight. Slink has also shifted from the bottom of the bed to the crook of her knees. I snap a quick picture, wanting to preserve this memory forever. I'm going to miss the crap out of her for the next two weeks.

During the entire drive up the coast, my mind keeps tumbling over the conversation. Is she right? Should I try to do something with my writing? It's not like I don't have plenty of money and a fair amount of passive income. I could keep myself going for a lot longer than most if needed. But even as I try to imagine what it would be like to write, complete a project, and get it published, my mind just rejects it. Sure, I may be an ok storyteller, but that doesn't mean I have what it takes to write a book and actually get it published. It doesn't mean anyone would actually want to read it. And if they did, what would they think? That thought is positively terrifying.

Hours later, I am still in my own head. I'm so out of it I actually startle when the director calls "cut" at the top of his lungs.

"Jason! What the hell are you doing? Did you not realize we were rolling?"

Fuck, no, I didn't. I look around the lights and camera equipment to where the director and other crew are all standing, staring at me like I've grown two heads.

"I'm sorry, guys, I need a minute. Can we take fifteen?" I don't even wait for a reply, I just get out of the area we're filming in. Without entirely thinking about it, I pull out my phone and text Alexis.

> **Jason:** Hey, beautiful. How are you feeling so far today? I miss you.

She takes less than a minute to reply.

> **Alexis:** Doing ok. The first 24 hours are always the worst. I miss you too. How is filming going? Are you guys on a break or something?

> **Jason:** Yeah, we're in between scenes. Can you send a pic? I'm missing my two girls.

A minute later, I'm graced with a picture of Alexis and Slinky all snuggled in our bed. What I wouldn't give to be there right now.

We exchange a few more texts before I head back. I feel a little better now that I've talked to her today, and everything feels more normal. The rest of filming goes a lot smoother.

CHAPTER 27

ALEXIS

Frantic.

That's all I am feeling at the moment.

Frantic to see my boyfriend after two loooong weeks apart.

Frantic to finish cleaning my apartment before my parents arrive.

Just frantic.

I'm finishing cleaning the toilet within an inch of its life when I hear my door open. "Honey! I'm home!"

With a shriek of delight, I run out of the bathroom and jump straight into Jason's arms. Well, that's what I was planning to do before he shoots an arm out and stops me.

"What?" The fuck, why is he laughing?

"I'm sorry, I don't mean to laugh. I want to hold you so bad, but Alexis. You're holding the toilet brush."

Oh.

I quickly hide it behind my back. "Shit, sorry, I was just so excited. Can we try that again?" He pauses, looking back toward the door, then back at me. I'm nodding frantically. "Mhmmm, yep. Like go back out in the hall, and I'll go back into the bathroom. And when you come in, I'll come running but without the disgusting cleaning utensil." I keep nodding, giving him my crazy eyes, so he knows I'm not fucking around.

"Ok, I'm going. But for the record, this is a little silly." He laughs and shakes his head. Going back out into the hall.

I race to the bathroom and drop the brush back into the toilet. I then take half a second to fluff my hair in the mirror.

The door opens and closes again. I hear him softly chuckle again before he calls out, "Honey! I'm home!" pause, "Again!"

I laugh, too, before I charge out of the bathroom and straight into his arms. We don't even kiss at first, we just hold each other, breathing each other in.

"Hi."

"Hey."

I tip my head back and pull him down for a kiss. Pure magic. It's sweet at first but turns hot quickly. His hands travel down to my ass, urging me to climb him like a tree and wrap my legs around his waist. Our tongues are basically battling for supremacy before he breaks the kiss to drag his lips and teeth down the side of my neck. I moan loudly at the sensations he's able to produce with just his teeth against my shoulder.

He takes us to the kitchen in a few strides, setting me down on the counter before stepping back. I nearly melt at the heat in his eyes, and I know mine are just as lustful.

"I am starving. I skipped lunch so I could drive straight here. So, after I eat you out, we're going on a date, and when we get back, I'll fuck you until you lose your voice. Sound good?"

Hot damn, I think I almost came from the dirty talk alone. I can't even vocalize my agreement; I need him so badly. So, I just nod and begin ripping off my clothing. He chuckles a bit before coming to help me. Within moments, I'm naked on the cool countertop, and his large hand on my chest is urging me back on my elbows.

He spreads my legs and then just looks at me like I'm the most beautiful thing he's ever seen. Before I can tell him to hurry up, he steps back up to the counter and gives me a searing kiss. Just as I start to pant again, he moves down my neck to my breasts. He spends a few minutes licking, nipping, and sucking on them, building the ache between my thighs from dull to a roar. I'm laid out fully on the counter, one hand in his hair, gripping hard, the other over my head, holding on to the counter edge for dear life.

"Jason!" I arch my back as he starts to move farther down, exactly where I need him.

"I know, baby, I'm going to make you feel so good. Just be patient."

I can't help the frustrated whine that escapes my lips as he pauses and pulls back again. He's hovering over my clit, blowing cool air on it, making me so damn wet and horny I can barely think. Just when I think he'll never stop teasing me, he finally, *finally* puts his mouth on me.

He starts with long, unhurried licks as if we have all the time in the world. I try to use my hips to urge him to move faster, harder, but he just evades me. I yank on his hair, frustrated, which only causes him to chuckle against my clit. Which, admittedly, felt good. Just not enough.

"Hollywood, you're killing me. Please, I'm begging. Please let me come!" There's so much desperation in my voice that I almost cringe. I sound so needy. But when I look down at Jason, I see the same desperation reflected back at me, and my insecurities melt away.

He lifts away from me again, and I think he's going to continue to edge me into oblivion when he says, "Baby, I can never say no to you. Hold on tight."

Then he sucks so hard on my clit that I see stars while slipping two fingers inside me and rubbing my G-spot. The pleasure is white hot, and I'm bent nearly in half, crying out his name while I come.

I'm in a literal daze as he sits me up and helps me dress. He shattered me and yet, somehow, put me back together at the same time.

It's not until we're walking out my door that I even realize I'm no longer on the counter. "Wait? What about you?" I tug on his hand, looking pointedly at the very large bulge in his jeans.

"I told you, Doc, I'm super hungry. We're going to eat, and then I'll let you take care of me."

This man.

Sometimes, he just does the darndest things.

Fuck, I love him so much.

He takes me back to Maison LaCroix. Which, by the way, don't make a joke about LaCroix Sparkling Water while you're there. They *do not* appreciate it.

Jason and I ate as if our lives depended on it, pigging out to the point that patrons were turning away in disgust. Luckily, neither of us noticed anyone snapping photos, so hopefully, we won't wake up to any fun, quirky articles about us in the morning. I spend our whole drive home palming him through his pants, making him crazy.

We barely make it into the elevator before we're lip-locked again. We fumble down the hall as we make our way to the door. After what feels like an eternity, he's able to unlock it, and we tumble in.

"Alexis, baby, I need you so bad," he hoists me up against him, and I can feel his rock-hard dick press into my belly. I need it in me now. In the blink of an eye, my clothes are off again, and he's half undressed. My back hits the cool hardwood of my floors;

we're both so horny, we can't even make it to one of our usual surfaces.

I don't feel it at first because it felt too good when he enters me the first time. The force of his thrust slides my body back bumpily, and a full second later is when I feel it. That burning sensation you get when you pinch your skin with friction.

"Ouch." I can't even contain my reaction. That fucking hurt.

Jason pulls back, concern marring his perfect features. "Shit baby, did I push in too fast? You felt so ready."

I'm shaking my head, "No, Jason, it's the floor. My skin got friction burned." I almost regret saying anything when I see the look of pure horror and regret on his face.

"Shit, Alexis, I'm so sorry. I didn't even think about that!" I slap my hand over his mouth to stop the spiral I can see building.

"Oh my god, Jason, stop. I'm ok, it's already starting to fade. I want you just as bad." I look around and spot his T-shirt. "Hand me your T-shirt and get back to it. I seem to remember you promised to fuck me so hard that I wouldn't have a voice." I clench my inner muscles around him to drive the point home. And just like that, the lust is back in his eyes, and he's reaching for his shirt.

T-shirt under me, he bends to give some more attention to my breasts. Once we're both panting again, he lines back up and thrusts in hard.

Instead of staying in place, the momentum of his thrust shoves my body back, sliding me a good foot into the living room. My head connects with the leg of the small table I have at the back of my couch. Then we hear something wobbling, then tipping, then rolling, causing us both to look up and watch in horror as my mother's favorite vase takes a dive. Are we cursed?

With agility I've only ever seen him exhibit on screen, Jason dives forward, catching the vase just before it hits the floor and smashes.

We both lay there for a moment in stunned silence.

And then a giggle escapes. And another. And another. Until I am laughing so hard tears are streaming out of my eyes, and my whole body shakes. After he sets the vase back where it belongs, Jason joins me in laughter.

After a minute, he gets up and pulls me up with him. But he doesn't stop there, he proceeds to throw me over his shoulder, ignoring my squeak of surprise, and smacks my ass. Fuck, did I like that?

"We're never doing it on the floor again, clearly." He says, humor still in his voice. His ass is level with my face, and I don't know what exactly puts the thought in my head, but the next thing I know, I'm taking a little nibble out of his right butt cheek.

His yelp of surprise sets off another round of giggling for me, which only gets worse when he tosses me on the bed.

"What was that for?" He pretends to be upset, rubbing his 'sore' ass.

I shrug, trying to look innocent while giggling. "I don't really know. Your lil' butt cheek just looked so juicy. I couldn't help it."

He twists around, attempting to look at his own ass as if he'll see what I see. When he turns back, the mood has shifted from playful to heated. "Listen here, you little shark, you're going to pay for that."

He lunges for me, and I shriek, pretending to try to get away. My upper body is halfway off the bed when he grabs my ankle and drags me over to his side. I can't help but continue to giggle. It's like when you and your friend are laughing in class, and the teacher gets mad at you for laughing, but for the life of you, you and your friend can't stop.

I'm still laughing as he flips me onto my stomach, then maneuvers my hips and knees until my ass is in the air.

It's not until I feel the sting of his hand on my left cheek that I can stop laughing and moan instead. Fuck, I liked that.

"Did you like that, Doctor?" He smooths a hand over the spot he just smacked, soothing the sting. I can only moan in response. Then his hand comes down on the other cheek, and my hips jolt back. Apparently, spanking makes me wet.

"Now, are we going to continue *without* further interruption?" His fingers are gliding through my wetness, teasing me as I begin to unravel again.

"Yes! Jason, I'll be good, I promise." I'm nodding, flexing my hands against the bedspread.

I feel him leave me, then hear the rip of a condom wrapper. I almost want to tell him not to bother. I know we're both clean and getting pregnant doesn't worry me. The fact that it doesn't scare me doesn't surprise me anymore. I've spent more time thinking about our future than I had for any past boyfriend combined. All I feel is excitement about the possibilities.

"Are you going to be good now and let me fuck you?" His voice is deep and silky, and I'm pretty sure we've both just unlocked a new kink for ourselves.

"Yes, Jason," I plead, squirming as he slowly pumps two fingers inside me.

Without warning, he slams home, causing me to cry out in pleasure. He's pumping hard, I can hear the smack of our skin as our bodies meet. In what feels like record time, I'm crying out as I come.

He slows a bit but doesn't stop or come himself. I'm basically incoherent at this point, my orgasm scrambling my brains.

"Jason," I wince, I'm so sensitive, but he won't let up the pace. "Jason, please, it's too much."

He leans over, his body covering my back; lips, and teeth snatching at my earlobe. A moan escapes from me when his teeth scrape against the soft skin.

"What did I tell you? You're going to come again. And then again and again until you can't speak. Do you understand?"

Oh fuck, why is that so hot? I find myself nodding, and he lifts himself back up. He adjusts my body, pushing my chest farther down into the mattress. The shift in angle isn't huge, but it somehow completely changes what I'm feeling as he continues to thrust, picking up his pace.

Soon I'm *chanting* his name. My voice is cracking, I might not completely lose it, but I will be hoarse for hours. One of his hands snakes around and pinches my clit. And I see stars for the second time tonight. The pleasure of release is almost too much. My limbs feel electrified. I cry out so loud that my ears are ringing. Behind me, I feel Jason buck erratically as he comes, shouting my name. As we both come down, he slowly flattens me out, his body lying on top of mine. His weight is comforting, instead of crushing, and suddenly I'm drowsy.

He leaves me briefly to take care of the condom before returning to bed. My muscles are liquid, I'm so sated I barely crack an eye when he literally hoists me up, so I'm no longer across the short way on the bed and am instead lying in his arms. One of his hands strokes my exposed upper arm.

"That," I say, poking him in his pec, his beautiful, beautiful pec that I am now wanting to bite, just like his ass. But I resist. Barely. "That was phenomenal, Hollywood." He chuckles into my hair, his breath tickling my scalp.

"Couldn't have said it better myself, Doc. Don't fall asleep, though, I'm not done with you yet."

And boy, he sure wasn't.

Chapter 28

Jason

I lost count of the number of times I made her come last night, but I think it was about five, maybe six. Seven? I had plans for more, but she fell asleep before I could wring another out of her. Making her come is, quite honestly, my life's work right now. It's all I think or care about.

I'm about to wake her up to get our day started right when she jolts awake, going from asleep to completely seated upright in half a second.

"Woah, Alexis. What's wrong, honey?" I sit up with her, running a hand over her shoulders. They're still sticky from sweat, maybe I can convince her to shower together. Usually, she kicks me out when she wants to shower. I 'disrupt her routine' too much.

"What time is it?" I smile. Her voice is rough. Not so bad that anyone would notice, but enough that *I* know why it sounds off. Not really sure what came over me last night, but it took our sex life to a new level. One where I'd like to stay.

"Uh," I glance down at my phone, "it's eleven. Why? Did you need to be at the hospital or something? I thought you had this week off?"

She ignores me completely, leaping, then briefly stumbling out of bed. She looks like a newborn calf on shaky legs. Clearly, not one hundred percent recovered from our fun last night. "Shit, shit, shit!"

Completely naked, she mutters to herself, moving about the room picking up clothes, and throwing them in the hamper. She continues this through to the living room too. Then it clicks; she was cleaning last night when I got home, her parents are likely due to arrive soon.

I hop up and find her in the bathroom, staring at the toilet, the brush still stuck in the bowl. When she hears me enter, she looks up, panic in her eyes. "They're due in three, maybe four hours. The apartment isn't even *clean* yet!" She grabs the brush and starts vigorously scrubbing, even though it looks sparkling already.

"Woah, there." I snatch the brush from her hands and place it in the holder. "You cleaned that last night. And aside from our clothes, the entire place is spotless. Let's shower first; that will make you feel better." She shoots me a dirty look as I herd her into the stall. I put my hands up, attempting to look innocent. "No funny business, I promise. I'll keep my hands to myself."

Not five minutes later, she's coming on my tongue, her front pressed against the shower's glass wall. Hopefully, now she'll be less stressed.

I wash up quickly and step out before she's even halfway through her shower routine. "Babe, I'm going to go get breakfast and coffees for us; I'll be right back. Don't stress, ok? I'll help you finish any cleaning you feel is still needed."

The shower muffles her voice, but I'm pretty sure she said ok.

I grin like an idiot the entire way to our favorite café; I can't even contain it once I'm inside, smiling and thanking everyone. I'm pretty sure I even thanked someone for just being in line.

When I get back, I'm pulled up short by something taped to her door. It's a white envelope, with "to Neighbor in Unit 505" written on it. I glance around to see if anyone is in the hall before grabbing it and stepping inside.

Alexis is already on the patio, a book in her lap. That's a good sign. I half expected to find her cleaning the toilet again. On second thought, when I reach the patio door, she's not actually looking at the pages. She's staring off into space, chewing on her bottom lip like it holds the secrets of the universe.

She looks up once I wave the coffee in her face and finally cracks a smile.

Before I broach the subject, I wait until she's had a few bites to eat and drank at least a quarter of her latté.

"What has you so worried about your parents visiting? I thought you wanted me to meet them?"

She closes her eyes and blows out a breath. Shit, maybe she doesn't want me to meet them?

"I *do* want you to meet them. But I'm scared too. My mom can be very intense. I know you feel like your mom is, but she honestly is chill compared to mine. I don't want her to freak you out and make you uncomfortable." She turns to me, her eyes actually watering.

I reach out my hand and tug on hers until she gets up and sits on my lap. Once she's settled, I tip her head back so she can see my face.

"Lex, there is nothing, and I mean *nothing*, your mom can do or say to freak me out. What do you think she might talk about that worries you?"

She shrugs at first, but I bounce her a bit, and she gives in. "I think she's going to ask about marriage and babies. Things you and I haven't really talked about yet."

"Well, then, let's talk about it. Do you want to get married?"

"Yes, but not right away. I still want us to find our rhythm." She pauses as if she's not sure she wants to say more. "I think we should at least live together first, right?"

I nod, glad we're on the same page on that front. It will make it much easier when I ask her to move in, and maybe I can even move up my timeline around that.

"Ok, so we're on the same page. Live together, then talk of marriage. What about kids?"

She chews her lip again, looking away before answering. "I want kids, two at least. But not for a while yet; I'm about to finish residency and hopefully become an attending at my hospital. Getting pregnant too soon could hurt my career growth."

That makes sense, "I also would like a couple of minis running around, but I'm in no rush." I grab her coffee and hand it to her, then take a sip of my own. "So, we're on the same page; your mother won't surprise me or freak me out." She sighs in relief and eventually relaxes against my chest. We sit there quietly for a few minutes, just sipping coffee and breathing each other in.

Then she notices the envelope. "What's that?"

"Oh yeah, I forgot. That was taped to your door when I got back." I hand it to her and sit back while she opens and reads the one-page note.

"Oh no..." Her eyes widen, a horrified look on her face. "Oh no, no, no, no, no!"

"What? What does it say?" I'm alarmed. What the fuck could a neighbor have written to freak her out like this? She just shakes her head and hands me the paper, abandoning my lap altogether.

I can't stop myself from laughing when I'm done reading.

Dear Neighbor in 505,

Hello, this is the neighbor that shares the wall with your bedroom. Did you know that? Our bedrooms share a wall. Because I sure did. While I am absolutely delighted that you seem to have a boyfriend or at least a regular bedfellow, I have to kindly ask that you refrain from the all-night sex marathons.

For a minute there, I thought maybe you both had resumed ordinary sexual exploits. You know, maybe one round of sex at night, at a normal time, and then sleeping until the next day. But no, last night, you were up until nearly five in the morning. Did you know that? FIVE IN THE MORNING.

While I applaud your stamina, I am begging *you to stop. I would really like to sleep at some point.*

All my best,

Your very tired Neighbor

"I cannot believe you are laughing!" Her eyes are wild, snatching the letter from me before storming inside. "This is a disaster!"

I quickly follow and find her sticking it under her pillow. Before she can move away, I wrap her up in a bear hug, resting my chin on her head. "It is not a disaster. Honestly, they sound jealous; they probably don't get any." She snorts at that, shaking her head slightly. "How about this? My unit is the coveted corner unit. I don't have neighbors who share walls with my bedroom. We can start having our all-night sex marathons there."

She laughs again, then turns in my arms, so her head rests against my chest.

"How do you always know the right thing to say?"

I shrug because, honestly, I don't know. "I just speak Alexis, I guess."

***

A few hours later, I've been banished back to my apartment. She wants to greet her parents and get them settled before we take them out to eat. Honestly, I think she just wants to try to talk to her mom first before she has a chance to speak to me.

Maybe another hour later, my door bursts open, with Alexis looking manic in the doorway.

"I'm moving in while they're here! I can't. I just can't." She brushes past me with a suitcase, going directly into my room.

"Forty-five minutes. My mom has been at my house for forty-five minutes, and it's already too much!" She throws her hands up, then grabs my arms and shakes me. "Do you know what she did? The *first* thing she did?"

I shake my head, a little afraid to speak honestly.

"She found my calendar where I track my period and started marking off the ovulation days with little hearts and stars! THEN, she showed me and said, and I QUOTE, 'honey, you need to pay better attention to when you are ovulating. You and

Jason aren't getting any younger. You'll want to start soon if you want any kids.' What the fuck? Like what the actual fuck!" She sucks in a breath, clearly gearing up for what happened next. "And then, I was in the bathroom, packing up my toiletries because, honestly, there is no way I'm staying there after *that*. She went into *my room* and, with the intuition of a fucking alien, found that note! And was reading it, OUT LOUD to my FATHER." She's shaking, or is that me?

"My father knows I have all-night sex marathons," she pauses and looks at me in horror. "My *father* knows I have all-night sex marathons!" She drops her hands and then throws herself on my bed, lying face down, shoulders slumped in defeat. Oh boy, this week should be fun.

CHAPTER 29

ALEXIS

I think I'm going to be sick.

Jason and I are walking down the hallway to my apartment, about to enter the lion's den.

His confidence that my mom couldn't scare him away does little to calm my nerves. I think what freaks me out the most is that I have no idea what my mom will do or say. I can't control her or predict her, and that uncertainty makes my chest tight.

Jason's hand squeezes mine just before we open the door and step through. It helps—just a little.

"Is that my one and only baby girl?" My mom calls from her and my father's room. Her head pops out, and she legitimately screams when she spots Jason.

"Oh my god! Bill! Stop taking a shit and get out here and meet your future son-in-law!"

The desire to turn around and leave is so strong, I actually start to move toward the door. But Jason just tugs me back and laughs as my mom practically sprints toward us.

Much like Martha, my mom doesn't hesitate to pull Jason into a hug. "Hello, Mrs. Masters; it's very nice to meet you." He doesn't hesitate to give her one right back.

"Oh Jason, you're practically family. Call me Cheryl." She pulls back and pinches his cheek like he's a kid visiting his grandma in the nursing home. A moment later, the toilet flushes, and we all hear my dad wash his hands. He's blushing slightly as he comes out of the bathroom, attempting to shut the door behind him discreetly. I don't even want to know what manner of foulness he dropped in there. And while he might be blushing a bit, I know my face is beet red.

Jason reaches out without hesitation and shakes my dad's hand. "Dr. Masters, it's nice to meet you as well." He flinches almost unperceptively as they awkwardly continue to shake hands. I just know they're doing that weird thing men do where they try to hurt each other through a handshake, to battle for dominance or something.

Apparently, Jason passes the test because my dad pulls away first and then slaps him on the back, hard. "No need to call me Dr. Masters. Bill will do just fine, son."

Before my parents can do or say anything worse, I'm charging for the door. "Come on! I'm hungry, and we have a dinner reservation we can't miss."

The car ride is awkward. But not because we don't have anything to say. Oh no. My mother hasn't stopped speaking for more than the time it takes to take a new breath. First, she regaled us with stories about how hard it can be to find a toilet while traveling and how it occasionally led to some hilarious situations with my father's IBS. She then immediately moved into talking about marriage and the perfect times and locations for outdoor California weddings. Had we thought about having ours in Napa? It feels overdone to her. But also somehow perfect? Or maybe a beach wedding? She then launched into the story about how she and my dad got married in a courthouse and how they immediately regretted the location and ended up renewing their vows in Costa Rica a year later. None of us could get a word in edge wise. Thankfully, we pulled up to the restaurant before she could get into the topic of babies or start sharing the horror story that was my birth. She *loves* telling that one.

While waiting for the host to take us to our table, Jason pulls me into his arms and presses a kiss to my temple. "Not freaked out in the slightest, Lex. Your mom is going to have to try harder." A distressed laugh escapes my lips as I rub my forehead into his chest. I slip my hands around him under his sport coat, pulling him tighter against me, wishing I could burrow into his skin. I don't care if my parents are watching or what the paps might get on camera; I just need his comforting body wrapped around mine as tightly as possible. He holds me tighter without hesitation.

The host comes, and before I let him go, I look up into his blue eyes and pinch his chin. I love his chin. "I love you," I whisper.

He smiles and pinches my chin back. "I love you too."

When I turn to follow the host, I find my mother staring at us, tears *flowing* down her cheeks. What have I done?

Surprisingly, she passes the dinner in a more normal state once she calms down. Asking Jason basic, non-invasive questions and actually giving him time to answer. I almost feel out of sorts, she's acting so level. Under the table, Jason keeps periodically squeezing my knee, comforting me.

As we're waiting for dessert, the topic of my birthday comes up.

"So, Jason, do you have any plans for Alexis' 30th this weekend? Bill and I had a few ideas, but I don't want to step on your toes if you have something already planned." I can't tell from the glint in my mom's eye if she wants him to have something planned or not. Before I can interject that we do not, in fact, have plans, Jason jumps in.

"Actually, Cheryl, I do." He just smiles when I look at him, surprised. "My parents have a place on Catalina Island and invited us to stay. I spoke with Lex's friends from the hospital, and they're all able to come as well. We'll have to get up pretty early Saturday morning to catch the ferry out of San Pedro to reach Two Harbors, but my parents said they'd have a big breakfast waiting for us when we arrive."

My jaw is on the floor. I had no clue he'd done any of this, let alone talked to the girls about their schedules. Hell, I only told him my birthday was coming up two weeks ago. Was he planning this while he was away filming?

He catches my awed look and gives me the smuggest smile I've ever seen. Oh, he's good. I pinch his arm, but without any force. After the initial shock rolls off, I find myself incandescently happy.

"Oh, did you hear that, Bill? That sounds wonderful! And we get to meet your parents?" My mom whacks my dad as if he wasn't already paying attention. He just nods and grunts like none of this was a big deal to him. But I know he'll pull me aside later and want to say something to me privately.

I pull out my phone and send a quick text to the group chat I have with Allison, Nique, and Tristan. Only slightly annoyed that they were able to keep this a secret.

Alexis: You hoes, how could you not tell me you were planning a party for me with Jason? You all made me think you were too busy to do something!

It takes less than ten seconds for their replies to roll in.

Kiki: Dammit! He was supposed to keep his lips sealed until you were on the ferry, and we jumped out of nowhere!

Allison: I'm sorry, sweety pie, but it was too good of a surprise to pass up. The look on your face when we told you we were all busy? [crying laughing emoji]

Tristan: I'd like the record to show that I was originally opposed, but was forced to comply.

Alexis: You're all lucky I love you guys, or I'd be dis-inviting you from this whole trip.

Allison: Noooooo! Don't do that! Phil has the kids this weekend AND I'm off. Don't take this me time away from me!!!!!! [sobbing GIF]

Kiki: I'll cut you if you leave me behind.

Tristan: Again, let the record show that I was always opposed to lying.

> **Alexis**: [repeating eye-roll emojis]

> **Alexis**: I'm getting dirty looks from my mother, so I gotta go. I guess I'll see you three on Saturday…….

Thankfully, before my mother can complain, our desserts arrive, and she's distracted by sugar.

***

Later in the evening, we're back at the apartment for one last glass of wine. My mom has kidnapped Jason to the kitchen, where she *needs help* opening a *rather pesky bottle*. Which is code for, *I want to talk to you without my disapproving daughter around*.

But it's ok because a little heart-to-heart in the kitchen is nothing after everything else she's pulled tonight. At least, I hope it's nothing.

Maybe I should go in there.

Before I can move, my father uses this as an opportunity to talk to me privately. He pulls me fully into the living room so we're out of earshot from the kitchen. I find myself frowning, it's not often that my father feels the need to exclude my mother from things. And now I'm a little concerned he doesn't want Jason to hear either.

"Sweetheart, you know I love and trust you, right?" He looks down at me from over his glasses, a slight crease in his brow. I feel like there's a big "but" coming.

"Yes?" it comes out more like a question, I have no idea where he's going with this.

"And I want you to know that I am so happy that you are happy with Jason. But I just want to make sure you don't get swept up in his glamorous life. New love can make you see everything through rose-colored glasses, and it's great, but it doesn't always last. You are nearing the end of residency; this is a crucial point in your career. I don't want you to lose sight of that because of a man."

I don't even know what to say, I just stare at him. Of all the things I thought he might say, I didn't expect him to question my ability to balance my life.

At my silence, he continues, "You know I married Lisa during my residency, and I was so caught up in the ups and downs of our relationship I almost lost sight of my career. I was so afraid of losing her, that I have into every selfish whim she had until I didn't know what I even wanted anymore. I just don't want you to make the same mistakes I did."

I sigh, closing my eyes briefly. I know he's just trying to protect me because he's my father, but I thought he understood that I wouldn't ever let someone get in the way of my career. I'm too driven.

"Dad, while I appreciate your concern, it's not needed. Jason knows how important my career is to me. We've had several discussions on our life goals and what takes priority. He would never push me to set anything aside in favor of our relationship. Just like I would never do that to him. Thank you, but I don't need you to worry."

He puts his hands up as if to calm me down, which honestly makes me more mad. "Alright, alright. But as your father, I just needed to get my worries off my chest. You do with them what you will. I love you, Bug."

And just like that, my childhood nickname disarms me entirely, and I'm no longer mad. Or at least, downgraded to frustrated. I begrudgingly smile and give him a hug. Just as we're separating, Jason and my mom enter with the wine and glasses. He's laughing at something my mom said, and she's grinning like she just won the lottery. My dad might be worried, but when I look at what we're starting to build? I'm not.

***

Much, much later, Jason and I are a tangle of limbs and sheets, one of his hands running up and down my spine. I'm sated and drowsy but can't quite sleep yet. I shift around a bit until I'm propped up on his chest and can see the smug smile on his face.

This time, I don't stop myself from leaning down and taking a little nibble out of his pec.

"Hey!" He slaps his hand over my mouth, a mock scowl on his face. I know my little love nips don't bother him; I can literally feel the evidence pressing against my hip. We're not sleeping anytime soon. "What was that for?"

I shrug, trying to look nonchalant. "Just wanted you to know how excited I am for this weekend. I can't believe you planned all this while wrapping your movie." He shrugs as if it isn't a big deal, but it is. It shows how much he pays attention and cares about me, that when he says 'I love you,' he means it. "I am a little worried about our mothers being in the same house, though. They'll either fall in love and gang up on us or initiate a Cold War." I pretend to shudder at the thought. "I'm not sure which would be worse."

He chuckles a bit, squeezing my arm. "I think they'll get along fine. I will concede that your mom might be a little more intense than mine, but their hearts are in the same place."

"Ha! So, you *do* admit that my mom is crazy!" I knew she'd freaked him out.

"Not crazy, just intense. She wants you to be happy, and a healthy relationship with me is a sign that you are, indeed, happy." He shrugs as if my mother's motivations are easy to understand.

I shake my head; this man is something else. How anyone could get through tonight with my mother and still have a favorable opinion of her is beyond me. I'm her daughter; I'm forced to unconditionally love her, crazy and all. But for Jason to be able to just roll with it? Well, it fills me up.

He lifts me up so he can quickly kiss me on the lips before settling us more comfortably in the bed. It's weird. This is the first night we've spent in his apartment. And while I'm glad I don't have to worry about my neighbor tonight or my parents, to be honest, I'm a little curious as to why we never hang out here. But just as I open my mouth to ask, I hear a snore. Jason is out, mouth open, and already drooling. I snap a picture and giggle to myself; this will be excellent blackmail material later.

Chapter 30

Jason

I may have miscalculated slightly.

I'm in the kitchen preparing a round of margaritas for the girls. They're all down by the pool, sunning themselves and enjoying the nice day out. After the giant breakfast we had earlier, I half expect them to all be asleep by the time I deliver the drinks.

My dad and Bill are on the patio, discussing his grill and the finer points of preparing steak. You know what any pair of old white dudes would care to discuss.

But no, I miscalculated.

Because right now, my mom and Cheryl are in the living room, whispering to each other and giggling quietly every minute or so. I'm honestly terrified of whatever it is they are cooking up.

To make matters worse, they've literally been like that since we arrived, which has made Alexis go from normal stressed to

"I can't stop sweating and pooping" stressed. And considering it's her birthday, I'm a little annoyed. Her mom should know that what she's doing is making her daughter anxious and cut it out. If I hadn't just met Cheryl, I would try to say something, but Alexis and I are finally finding our footing, and getting into an argument, justified or not, with her mother is not advisable.

So instead, I go for my own mother.

She'll be easier to break anyway.

"Hey, Mom? Can you come to the kitchen quick? I can't find that thingy you use to grate the lime." I start banging a few drawers and cabinets for good measure. The whispering stops, and I hear my mom say she will be right back. Thank god Cheryl is staying put.

When my mom comes through the entryway, she's smiling so wide I feel like it must hurt. Damn, I really hate that I'm going to rain on her parade now, but Alexis is my priority today.

"Honey," she says exasperated, pointing to the zester already in my hand.

"Sorry, Mom, I just needed to talk to you quick," I pause and listen, hoping Cheryl has stayed out of earshot, "without Lex's mom," I say that part quietly, just in case. Understanding dawns on my mom's face, and she rounds the island so I can keep my voice low.

"So, I'm so glad you are hitting it off with Cheryl, and Alexis is too. Or she will be. Once she stops agonizing over the fact that you two seem to be planning something. It's her birthday, and I really want her to relax and enjoy the weekend, but she absolutely won't if she thinks you are cooking something up together." My mom nods, not even trying to deny what I'm saying.

"It would help a lot, I think, if you both go out to the pool, but you know, did your own thing. Like maybe read quietly? Or engage with at least one other person?"

She pats my arm. "Yes darling, I hear you. We'll come out to the pool in a minute. But can I just show you one thing?" I sigh but nod. If listening now means she'll stop plotting with Cheryl, I'm all ears.

"When your sister was born, and we knew we wouldn't have any more kids, your grandmother took a necklace that had been in the family for generations and had it turned into rings. She said, 'people don't wear this kind of jewelry anymore, and I want to give my grandchildren something they'll use.'" From her pocket, she pulls out a small box, and inside are two rings. There must have been multiple types of stones in the original piece because one of the rings has a sapphire center stone, and the other has something else, amethyst, maybe? Both were flanked by two smaller diamonds on each side. They weren't giant or ostentatious and look like they could be easily paired with any kind of wedding band. Honestly, they're exactly what I would look for in a ring.

"She wanted you and Isla to be able to have these when you got married. I just wanted you to know that I have these *if* you want to use one. But I understand if you want to pick something out yourself, or maybe with Alexis, so you won't hurt my feelings. Just know these are here."

"Thanks, Mom. I'll be honest, it's definitely on my mind, but Alexis and I both agreed we'd live together first, *then* talk about marriage. So, for now, just keep them safe."

A few minutes later, I'm hauling the tray of margs down to the pool. Allison and Tristan are both passed out; Allison is even snoring. Nique is swimming laps in the pool like she's training for the Olympics. And Alexis?

Well, she's sitting on a lounger, book in hand, staring daggers at her mother, who is at this point also by the pool with a book of her own. My mother is nowhere to be seen, but I'm sure she'll pop out eventually.

I set the drinks down, grab two and join my girl.

Once we're situated, her back to my chest, me holding her drink for her, so she can sip and hold her book at the same time; I try to broach the subject. "I talked to my mom."

"About?"

"Well, about whatever scheming she and your mom are doing. I asked her to cut it out and save it for another day that isn't your birthday."

She relaxes. Slightly. "Did she agree?"

"Yes, she understands that you just want to enjoy the rest of this weekend and respects that. I'm sure they'll exchange numbers and continue plotting, but it won't be where we can see or hear them." I tip my head forward to place a kiss on her head, hoping she'll chill out now.

It takes a few minutes, and some healthy sips of her margarita before she finally relaxes into me and starts reading for real.

***

It's mid-afternoon, and the group has disbanded to get cleaned up and ready for dinner. Alexis is in the shower, and I'm about to join her, but I need to check my phone first. Ten missed calls. All from my agent. Fuck me. I know what he wants, but I can't handle it right now. I don't have an answer for him, and I won't before Monday, so he needs to just chill.

I'm incredibly frustrated when I step into the bathroom. I almost turn around and leave, my mood is so foul, but Alexis' voice stops me dead in my tracks.

"Oh, Jason!" Shit, she sounds sexy right now. "I believe as the birthday girl, I get to request orgasm services from a certain someone. I find myself in need of one. Now."

You don't have to tell me twice. I am stripped and in the shower with her in record time.

She's rinsing something out of her hair when I get in, so I wait patiently for her to be done; I don't want to be responsible for disrupting her routine. When her eyes finally flutter open, I can't help but take a moment to appreciate them. Perfectly shaped lashes that fan out elegantly and a shade of green that only nature can produce. I get lost in these eyes.

"What?"

"Nothing, I just love looking at you." I reach out and cup her cheek, pulling her close with my other hand and claiming her lips. Fuck, how does she always taste so good? A sigh escapes her lips as I press her against the shower wall.

I keep moving, trailing across her cheek and down the side of her neck, biting and kissing as I go. I can never get enough of her soft skin. I'm about to give her a hickey on the spot where her shoulder meets her neck when she's suddenly pushing me away.

"Don't you dare give me another hickey. It's bad enough everyone gives me shit about it at work, I don't need my parents seeing it." She gives me a stern look.

"What if I give you a hickey somewhere else, where they won't see?" Don't ask me why, because I honestly don't know, but I really enjoy giving her hickeys.

"Nope. Not this time. Because one turns into three, and knowing my mother, she'll somehow intuit that I have them and make me show her." Honestly, I wouldn't put it past that woman.

I pretend to pout but acquiesce; I'll do anything she asks me.

I resume my slow journey south over her collarbone to her tits. My balls tighten when I notice her nipples are already hard despite the steamy environment. I begin sucking and nipping at them ravenously. Suddenly, I need to be in her now. I slip one hand between her legs, rubbing my thumb on her clit just the way she likes. While my thumb circles, two fingers slowly pump in and out, with each pass, they rub her G-spot. Without fail, this gets her going within minutes.

"Jason! Yes, yes, right there. I'm close, so good. Fuck, how do you do that?" She's tipped her head back against the tiles, eyes squeezed shut. I can feel my smile turn wolfish; I love I make her crazy.

I'm about to lift her up and slam home when I realize my critical error. "Fuck, Alexis, I forgot condoms." Before I can even finish my sentence, she's shaking her head. "Doesn't matter, it'll be fine this time. Thanks to my mother, I know I don't ovulate for a few days."

Her eyes immediately fly open, looking at me in complete shock. "Did I just say that?"

"Unfortunately, yes." Another moment of silence.

Shit, I can see her starting to pull away. I am absolutely not going to let her comment about her mom end our fun. I drop to my knees, hook one of her knees over my shoulder and get my lips on her clit. Within moments, she's panting again and rolling her hips in rhythm with my mouth. Just as she's about to come, I pull back.

Her mewl of protest quickly becomes a moan as I lift her up and wrap her legs around my waist. I'm poised at her entrance, teasing her a bit until she's writhing in my arms, demanding I get on with it. Damn, she can be so pushy. I love it.

We both groan as I slowly slide in. Her wet heat envelops me, and I have to actively try not to spill my load immediately.

When we accidentally went without a condom all those weeks ago, I hadn't really paid attention to how different it felt.

Now though?

Pure bliss. My cock won't want to wear one ever again.

I'm just starting to find the right rhythm when there's a sharp knock at the door.

Alexis gasps, and we both freeze. Who the fuck is interrupting?

"Alexis, honey? It's Mommy." Cheryl's muffled voice travels through the bathroom. We both look at each other with probably identical horrified looks on our faces, which would be funny in any other circumstance.

"Yes, Mom?" I drop my head to her chest, trying desperately to not laugh or make a sound.

"Wondering if you know where Jason is? His father needs help with the grill, but we can't seem to find him."

Fucking Dad. He's a goddamn grill master; what would he need me for?

"Oh, um." Alexis hesitates, probably because she doesn't want to lie, but also doesn't want her mom to know what we are doing in here. "You know I have no idea where he is. I thought he said something about taking a phone call?"

At this moment, a wicked idea pops into my head that I can't shake. There's no way I'm letting Cheryl cockblock me.

I begin to move again, slow and steady. Alexis' nails dig into my shoulders, and I can see she's trying to tell me to stop fucking moving with her eyes, but I pretend not to understand. My lips and teeth trail up and down her neck, causing her to shiver.

I almost think her mom has left when the door handle rattles. Thank fuck I locked it when I came in.

"Alexis? Can I come in? I want to talk to you about something."

Poor Alexis, she's simultaneously in complete panic while her orgasm begins to loom. I can feel her inner muscles begin to clench me tightly. Fuck, that feels so good.

"Mom!" Her voice comes out as a squeak as she tries to sound normal while pleasure courses through her veins. "I'm in the middle of my... my hair routine. I'll be out soon and can talk to you then."

There's a pause on the other side of the door. "Fine, I'll wait in my room."

As soon as it feels safe, I begin to pump in earnest. She moans and tips her head back again.

"Yes! Jason, that's so good." She bites her lip, starting to tense as her orgasm rolls through. I follow her immediately, feeling the fire in my balls and legs as I pump inside her. We rest there a moment, both catching our breaths.

Slowly, I pull out and look down, feeling a sharp thrill as I see my cum seep out of her. Why is that so hot?

She pokes me sharply in my pec, pulling my attention to her face. Uh oh. She looks pissed. No, livid.

"You. Are. So. Fucking. Lucky." My balls shrivel a bit. "You better rub my feet for an hour *each* to make up for that."

"Yup, whatever you want, babe. I'll rub them for two hours each if you want." I did not think this all the way through.

She just rolls her eyes and grabs her facewash, turning her back to me. Clearly, I'm dismissed.

As I exit the bathroom, I try to move slowly and quietly in case Cheryl or my dad are lying in wait. Once I know the coast is clear, I throw on my clothes and go looking for my dad.

Turned out that all my dad wanted was to show me the cake they had gotten for Alexis and get my approval. Dinner passes quickly, everyone enjoying the food and cake. Alexis even looks delighted when we light the candles and sing to her. We're incredibly off-key, but she's smiling so big, it doesn't matter. This is what birthdays are about, being surrounded by your loved ones, sharing meals and stories.

***

It's late, everyone has gone to bed, but Alexis and I are still by the fire pit, snuggled under a blanket. I gave her not only the required foot rubs, but I also gave her a back rub. And no funny business.

It's time for her present, but I'm suddenly very nervous about giving it to her. What if she hates it?

She yawns for the second time and begins her eye-rubbing routine. Every night as she gets sleepy, she rubs each eye twice. I don't think she realizes she does it, but I find it fucking adorable. It's the surefire way to know that she needs to go to bed.

So, I put on my big kid pants and grab her gift from under the deck lounger we're on.

"This is for you, baby; happy birthday."

"Jason, you didn't have to get me anything! This whole weekend is plenty." She says this while simultaneously ripping open the box, clearly eager to see what I got her. When she pulls the item out, she goes quiet and I immediately start to sweat.

I shift uncomfortably, wondering what the hell she's thinking.

"It's, uh, it's all my short stories I've ever written. I had them bound. For you." Shit, she still hasn't said anything, and my insecurities over my writing are starting to invade. "If you don't like it, I'll just take it back. Maybe this was a dumb—"

One of her hands gently covers my mouth, stopping me from completing that sentence. She turns so that she's straddling me, and I have a full view of her face. Tears are slipping from her eyes, and all at once, I'm alarmed and relieved.

"Jason. This is legitimately the best gift I have ever gotten. I don't just like it. I *love* it. And if you try to take this back, I will cut off your dick." I legit flinch at her threat, no one with a penis wants their junk cut off. Even if it's an adorable brunette, who you love, doing it.

"Ok." I smile shakily. "There are fifteen of them. Some are from high school, so don't judge them too harshly."

She clutches the book to her chest before leaning forward and pressing her lips to mine. The kiss is short and sweet, but it fills me with the warm fuzzies.

Any writer will tell you; it can be incredibly difficult to let someone read your work. It's like taking a piece of your soul and handing it over. Even if it's someone you love, maybe especially when it's someone you love. At the moment, I'm equally excited and terrified of what she'll think.

She yawns again, and I know it's time to call it.

"Alright, sleepyhead. Let's go to bed. We have our kayaking tour tomorrow, and you need to be well-rested."

She doesn't fight me as I stand up, pulling her with me. She then forces me to pick her up and carry her all the way to bed.

No complaints here. I love carrying her. Taking care of her.

CHAPTER 31

ALEXIS

We said goodbye to my parents this morning, who left for a Mediterranean cruise. I won't say I necessarily cheered when the door closed behind them, but I definitely thrust my fists into the air in victory.

In all honesty, my mom did calm down a lot and was almost a normal human being by the end of the weekend. Hopefully, this is a sign that she will remain chill.

Ha. No, she's just saving up her energy.

Since I'm about to start three overnight shifts followed by two days on-call, Jason and I are settling in for a quiet day watching movies.

I'm in the kitchen popping our first round of popcorn when his phone goes off. I watch as he pulls it out, grimaces, and shuts off the ringer. It's the fourth time I've watched him do that today. Not to mention the number of times he did that all weekend. I've seen his call screen; I know it's his agent. What I don't understand is why he won't talk to the guy, clearly, he has something to say.

My first instinct is to say it's not my business and let him talk about it if he wants. Fuck that. He's the first person I want to talk things out with, and after that gift he gave me, I *know* he feels the same. We're barreling toward a lifetime together, so we need to start talking about the stuff that scares us, not just the fun stuff. My stomach clenches. I'm nervous about bringing it up, but I know if I don't, I'll regret it.

Popcorn in hand, I join him on the couch. He helps me get settled under the blanket, and I take the leap just as the opening scenes come on screen.

"Are you going to answer Steven next time he calls?"

Silence.

I think he didn't hear me for a second, but when I turn my head to look at him, he's scowling at the TV. Shit, maybe I shouldn't have said anything. But no, this is what being in a relationship is about. I can't back down at the first sign of resistance.

"I understand why you might not want to talk about it, but Jason, my job as your girlfriend is to be your sounding board. Not just when you're happy about something, but when you're struggling too." I take a breath and pause; at his silence, I push on.

"I know you said you didn't like anything he's brought you in the past, but there are probably new options by now. Maybe you should hear him out?"

Jason briefly closes his eyes, pinching the bridge of his nose. Then he blows a breath out and turns to look at me finally.

"I've looked at everything he sends me. Nothing is speaking to me. And he just won't leave me alone about it." He takes my hand in both of his and begins playing with my fingers. "I honestly don't know what to do."

I let out a breath, incredibly relieved that we're finally talking about it.

I twist around so that I'm seated facing him directly, the movie can go fuck itself for all I care.

"Jason," I wait for him to look at me again. "I want you to listen to everything I have to say and not interrupt. Do you think you can do that?"

He nods, his frown deepening.

Here goes nothing.

"I finished your short stories last night. They were wonderful." He opens his mouth, and I cut him off, "nope, you promised to let me finish." I wait for his mouth to close again before continuing.

"You weren't wrong that there were some structure and grammatical issues in some of your pieces from high school, but the storytelling and the stories themselves? I loved every minute of them. Now, I'm not saying you need to pursue your writing, but I want you to know that you *are* good; the praise you got from teachers was warranted. As for acting? Maybe you need a break. You've said it several times, nothing is speaking to you right now, and maybe that's a sign that you need to take a step back. I know, I know. You've been off since wrapping your last movie, but it's been with Steven looming in the background, pressuring you into picking your next project. Not to mention your parents asking you constantly too. I can't help but think that you'll find your footing again if you take an official break and have time to really think about what you want to do next without all these outside pressures. Babe, I want you to be happy, and sometimes it just doesn't feel like you are. I love you, and I'm here."

I can't look him in the eye; I'm so nervous that he's going to explode at me like the last time I tried to talk about this.

When he remains silent, I chance a look. He's back to staring at the TV, but his expression is more contemplative than angry or frustrated. Maybe I wasn't entirely off base here.

"I honestly don't know, Lex. What you're saying makes sense, but the thought of telling everyone that I'm taking a break from acting also scares me. I don't want to take a few months off and come back to find that no one wants to work with me anymore." He focuses back on me, and I can see the anxiety and indecision in his eyes. I wish I could make it easier for him. "But I'll think about it." I smile and pull him close for a chaste kiss.

"That's all I can ask for. Now let's get this movie marathon going."

We both settle in and spend the hours leading up to my night shift in perfect companionship.

Chapter 32

Jason

With my days spent spinning my wheels while Alexis sleeps, I really took time to consider what she said. At first, I wanted to completely disregard what she was suggesting, but I forced myself to listen. It's scary to think about taking a break from your career after two decades, but I don't know what else to do at this point.

I'm tempted to call my parents and ask them if they've ever felt this way, but I can't seem to hit the call button. I crave their advice, but I'm also terrified of disappointing them. So, I'm paralyzed on that front.

Instead, I hang out with Slinky during the day, keeping us quiet so that Alexis isn't woken up. And at night, I sleep in her bed, wishing she was next to me. Slinky doesn't let me sleep alone, though, so it isn't too bad. It's funny, aside from when her parents were here, we've never stayed at my place. And it's not from a lack of not wanting to share it; I just don't care to. Alexis' apartment quickly became home for me, and now when I'm in my apartment, all I can think is that we should just move in together. I don't want us separated any more than necessary, and having two apartments leaves that open. Once she's off these shifts, I'll talk to her about it.

I hear the door open and close just as I'm serving breakfast.

"Do I smell bacon?"

"You sure do, Sweet Cheeks." I smile, feeling that familiar clench in my chest when she enters the kitchen. Doesn't matter how long it's been since I last had eyes on her; I always miss her when we're apart. "Take a seat; I'll bring you a plate."

She sits at the table, scooping up Slinky, who is delighted to be getting chin scratches. Alexis sighs when I set the plate full of bacon, scrambled eggs, and French toast. "This looks amazing. Come here, I need a kiss." You don't have to tell me twice.

I lean down and capture her lips with mine. I keep it quick, knowing she's super hungry and that if I go any longer, we'll be ignoring our food in favor of getting each other naked. Food first, sex later.

"How was your last overnight? Nothing crazy, I hope?"

She shrugs, mouth full of bacon and eggs. Even with a mouth full of food, she turns me on. Goddamn, she's cute.

"It wasn't too bad. We had a bad car accident come in, but luckily, we were able to get both patients stable." She takes another bite of food, then washes it down with orange juice. "Honestly, I'm just dreading these next couple of days of on-call.

I hate when I have a short stint in overnight and then am on-call. My sleep schedule is always super off for a while afterward, and it seems like a dumb system. Maybe once I'm an attending, I can get them to change that."

"Have they asked you yet? To be an attending in a few months."

She shrugs again. "Not officially, but it's not surprising. I think they're waiting to see if I start looking for other positions before making any moves. I'm not overly worried. If they don't want me, plenty of other hospitals need a good ER doctor." Her confidence never ceases to amaze me.

Once we've inhaled our food, I send her to the bathroom to shower while I clean up the dishes. Usually, we split cooking and washing more equitably, but I can tell she's exhausted. She has about five hours off before she's officially on-call, and I want her to rest as much as possible.

We're cuddling on the couch; Alexis is drifting when my phone dings.

> **Steven:** Dude, you've dodged me long enough. I'll be at Holden Forrest's party tonight. You need to come so we can talk. This isn't a request.

Fuck. Steven's a top agent and a busy man. Clearly, I've tested his patience to the breaking point. And while I would love to continue to ignore him, I know I need to grow up and face this head-on.

"Who was that?" Her voice is sleepy, rumbling through my chest, "I felt your whole body tense."

"It was Steven. He wants me to find him at a party tonight and talk." I sigh, wishing I could skip.

"Have you decided what you want to do?" She rubs my chest, clearly trying to soothe my distress.

"Kind of. I think you're right; I need to take a break. But it's still scary to think about. I just know that I need to get him off my back for a while so I can get my head straight."

She nods against my chest, then plants a kiss over my heart.

"Will you go with me tonight?"

"I'm on-call; I really shouldn't."

"I know, but I promise I won't drink, and I'll leave the second you get a call. Holden's place is actually pretty close to the hospital, so it won't take us long to get there if you're called in."

When she hesitates, I put on my best puppy dog eyes, not above begging. "Please? I really need you there with me; I don't think I'll have the courage to tell him without you."

She blows out a breath and stays silent for a moment, chewing on her lip. "Fine, but we're leaving the second I get a call. Even if you're in the middle of telling Steven where he can shove it."

I can't help but chuckle, such a way with words. "Absolutely. Thank you."

Chapter 33

ALEXIS

The bass is bumping when we arrive. In fact, the music is so loud, I'm not sure how Jason or Steven plan on talking to each other.

A wave of nerves rush down my spine. My volume on my on-call phone is all the way up, and I have the vibrations turned on. I should be fine, but I can't help but be anxious about missing a call. Normally, I just stay home and anxiously watch my phone. I know many doctors just go about their lives when on-call, but I've never been able to do that.

It takes us nearly two hours to find Steven. By the time we found him, my blood was boiling. Who tells a client to meet them at a party and then not make it super easy to find each other to chat? To make it worse, we found him on a couch with two women on his lap, petting his head. Pig.

When he sees Jason, he stands and gives us an oily smile. Maybe it's because I know Jason doesn't like him that much, but I instantly don't like him.

"Jason!" He has to yell over the music. "It's been too long. What's up, man?"

They do a handshake-back slap combo, and I can't help but notice that Steven is ignoring me. Probably on purpose. I barely resist rolling my eyes.

"I've been ok, man. This is my girlfriend, Dr. Alexis Masters." He pulls me into his side, with a hard edge to his voice. I guess he noticed Steven purposefully not look my way too. The dick gives me a polite nod and then turns his attention back to Jason. Ass.

"So, you've been dodging my calls. We really need to get you signed for your next movie. Did you look at the one I sent you this afternoon? I really think *Primogenesis Fallout* is perfect for you. The perfect mix of action and feelings." I almost snort. What kind of a movie title is that? Is primogenesis even a word?

"I don't know, man; I don't love the script. I actually—"

Steven immediately cuts him off. "Jason. As your agent, I gotta say, you're taking too long to pick a project. So, what if the script isn't perfect? You're Jason Adams, have them change it. The director and producers really want you. They won't take no for an answer."

To my horror, I see Jason begin to waffle.

"Maybe if I met with them? I'm still not convinced."

What the hell is he doing? We came here to tell Steven to fuck right off, not to let him convince Jason to do a new project. I'm opening my mouth to say something when the music suddenly goes quiet, and I hear it.

Fuck. Me.

My on-call phone is blaring.

Shit, shit, shit, shit, shit.

I pull it out and nearly puke when I see that I have eight missed calls. How did I not feel it go off? Oh my god.

I don't even look at Jason before I take off, aiming for the front door. I'm fuming, not only at him but also at myself. I *knew* I shouldn't have come to this fucking party.

As soon as I'm outside, I answer the call.

"Hello, Dr. Masters speaking."

"It's Nurse Halloway. We have a multi-car accident coming in. It sounds like one patient is coming in with a partial amputation. Dr. Jordan is asking how long it's going to take for you to get here?"

"Shit, I'm on my way. Ten minutes, fifteen tops. Please let Dr. Jordan know I'll be there asap."

I'm hanging up when Jason joins me, keys already in hand.

He opens his mouth but snaps it shut when I hold my hand up. "Don't. I don't want to hear anything right now. Just get me to the hospital. We'll talk later."

Thankfully, he listens, and we spend the car ride in silence.

I sit there the whole time trying to reign in my feelings. I need a clear head right now; the night sounds like it's going to be a long one.

I don't even say anything to him when he pulls up to the hospital entrance. I just jump out and run in. Dr. Jordan is the lead attending for the ER. If I have any chance of becoming an attending here, I may have just blown it. Shit. Fuck!

***

Hours later, I feel dead on my feet. Dr. Jordan gave me a look when I entered the ER but kept any comments to herself since we had patients to treat. At around seven this morning, my phone pinged with a meeting request for a disciplinary meeting tomorrow. I'm so screwed.

The whole night, when I wasn't treating patients, all I could think about was that my dad was right. I let myself get swept up in our relationship and ignored my duty to this job, to my patients. And now I might lose it.

I don't answer any of Jason's texts or phone calls. Instead, I order a car and spend the whole ride trying not to cry. Pretty sure the driver wished they hadn't accepted my ride request.

I'm dreading what I have to do next.

Chapter 34

Jason

I spent the whole night in emotional agony. Not only am I disappointed in myself for not telling Steven off right away, I'm absolutely devastated that Alexis missed so many calls. The look on her face when she got out of my car. I never want to see that again.

I'm sitting on her couch, feeling sick to my stomach, when I hear her come in.

I'm off the couch like a rocket, heading for the door. Maybe once I see her, I'll stop feeling like the world is ending.

But when I see her face, I just know.

"Fuck, Alexis, baby, I'm so sorry." She holds her hand up; her eyes are cold and face blank. No, no, no, no, no!

"Jason, I can't do this right now." She moves past me into the living room, looking absolutely defeated. I follow her because I can't not. When she feels me follow, she whips around, fire and anger blazing.

"You nearly cost me my job last night. In fact, you probably cost me my spot as an attending!"

"I know, I'm so, so sorry, babe. I—" She cuts me off, not done handing my ass to me.

"I already have a disciplinary meeting with the lead attending tomorrow morning because of this. My dad was right! I let you sweep me up into this little bubble where only you and I existed. I let you convince me to go to that party when *I knew* I should stay home!"

She throws her hands up, diving them into her hair, pulling on the strands in distress.

"And you know what? That's not even the worse part!" My throat is closed up, my chest is tight. I can't even think of what to say or how to stop the words from tumbling out of her mouth.

"The worst part is that you were going to give in. You couldn't stand up for yourself when it mattered most. And I can't be a life partner to someone who is miserable but won't do anything about it."

She turns away again, wrapping her arms around her torso. I want so badly to reach out and hold her. But I can't; I know what happens next.

"You made me put you first on a night when you knew I couldn't. I'm an ER doctor, I'm not a normal person. I have a duty to heal people on the worst day of their lives, and sometimes that means I have to put my family second. I thought you understood that."

"I do, Alexis. I swear." This time I do reach out, gently turning her around to face me. I wish I hadn't though, because the look on her face stops my heart.

"I need you to leave, Jason. Leave your key. This is over."

I swallow the bile that's building in my throat. Tears slipping down my cheeks; I didn't even feel them coming on.

"Just like that? You're ending this? Ending us?"

"Yes."

So final. Her voice sounds dead. I feel hot, suddenly angry that she's just giving up, without a real fight. I want to yell. I want us to get in each other's faces and, fuck, I don't know, work it out? It doesn't have to be pretty, it just has to end with us still together.

But when I look at her now, I know nothing I say will change things. Her face is perfectly blank, but her arms are wrapped around torso, as if she's holding herself together. I take a half step toward her, but she shakes her head hard.

So, I pull out my key ring and unclip her extra key, setting it on the little table that was featured in our all-night sex marathon only weeks ago. I don't want to leave, but I don't know what else to do that won't just make things worse.

Her shoulders begin to shake, and it kills me that I did that.

"I'm so sorry," I whisper one last time before leaving.

When I reach my apartment, I collapse against my door. Sobbing.

I think I just lost the love of my life.

Chapter 35

Alexis

The disciplinary meeting went about as expected. I didn't even bother trying to defend myself or explain; I should have known better. Dr. Jordan wrapped up the meeting by saying, "Now, Alexis, I have to tell you that we were going to offer you a position as an attending. But after this, we're going to have to seriously reconsider. You are a good doctor, and I want you on my team, but only if I can rely on you."

"You can rely on me, I promise. This will never happen again." I left the meeting feeling shattered.

And when I got back to my apartment, I fell apart. Sobbing so hard I almost made myself sick. Not only have I lost the only man I've ever loved, I might lose my dream job too. Slinky tries to comfort me, but it's not enough.

That was a week ago. And I still feel raw.

Every time I look at my bookcase, I miss him. Every time Slinky outdoes herself in ridiculousness, I want to turn and find him there, laughing along with me. My whole body aches without him—his laughter, his kindness, his drugging kisses. Never in my life have I felt this lost.

But the thought of walking down the hall and knocking on his door repulses me. Not because I don't still love him, but because I *do*. If he can't figure out how to advocate for himself now, what will happen five years from now, when I've had a baby and the tabloids won't shut up about not "losing the baby weight" fast enough? What happens if they start to go after our kids? Is he going to let complete strangers walk all over us without a fight?

Part of me knows I'm being unfair. That a good partner would support him, help him grow and learn from this. But all I can think about is how my dad did that. How he tried, over and over again, to help his first wife through crisis after crisis. Every time she promised it would be the last, that she would do better. And every time she let him down. And his career and patients suffered. He was barely able to keep his career afloat after the dust settled post-divorce. I don't want to wake up ten years from now and realize I've done the same thing.

To try to block out the pain, I've come to every shift thirty minutes early and left thirty minutes later. Anytime someone needs help, I jump in immediately. All of my energy is focused on being the best doctor I can be. Because if I don't, if I let myself relax for even a moment, I'm worried I'll break.

I have to prove to them that I have what it takes; I can't lose this too.

Eventually, it will get easier, right?

CHAPTER 36

JASON

It's been two weeks since Alexis ended things, and I've barely left my apartment. I'm drowning without her, and I have no idea how I'm going to go on.

My mom and dad have called daily. Steven is pissed, but he can go die in a hole for all I care. I can't even bring myself to talk to Isla, who is usually the first family member I turn to. I'm unmoored, drifting with no direction.

When my phone rings, I almost don't even bother to look. Whoever it is, I don't feel like talking. But I force myself to look, just in case it's Alexis.

No.

But it is someone I didn't expect.

Vanessa.

I haven't spoken to her in months since we broke up. I feel incredibly guilty, but I wasn't sure she would want to talk to me after the news broke about her being in recovery.

Before I can talk myself out of it, I answer.

"Hello?"

"Hi, Jason, it's Vanessa." Pause, she sounds nervous. "Do you have a few minutes to talk?"

I suppress a sigh; I don't really want to do this, but I owe it to her.

"Yeah, I can talk. But first, can I say something?"

"Sure..." she sounds hesitant. I don't blame her.

"I just want to say that I'm sorry." I take a deep breath and keep going. "I didn't see how much you were struggling, and it kills me that I blew you off. I didn't see it, and I'm so sorry. I just want you to know that if I had realized how hard you were spiraling, I would have tried to help. I hope you can forgive me."

She sighs on the line, but I can't tell if it's an 'I'm relieved' or 'I'm annoyed' sigh.

"Jason, you have nothing to be sorry for. That's my job. Wait, let me finish. If you interrupt, I'll never be able to get this all out."

I almost laugh, she still knows me well enough to know that I don't usually let others take the blame off my shoulders. But she sounds shaky, and I need to listen.

"I know you probably saw the news when it broke, but I'm an alcoholic. I've always struggled with my mental health since I was young, but as I got older, it became unmanageable. I would have really good months and then really low ones, and I self-medicated with alcohol. I reasoned with myself that because it was a legal substance, I wasn't really abusing it. But the reality is that I was. That night we broke up, I was on a five-day bender, and if we hadn't had that fight, I might not have been caught. Or I could be worse than I am now. This didn't get out into the media, but I tried to drive after. I didn't get far before being pulled over, and I didn't hurt anyone, but I could have. It was the wake-up call I needed, and I've been in treatment since." She pauses, sucking in a shaky breath. I can only imagine how hard this must be for her.

"I need you to understand that I never wanted to hurt you. I was spiraling about the project I was on, my stepfather, and how lost and alone I felt. I wanted to destroy my life rather than feel numb. No one but me could have stopped it from happening, and I am trying my best to own my mistakes. I hope *you* can forgive me."

"Of course, Vanessa. You don't even have to ask; I forgave you the minute I learned you were struggling. I actually talked to my girlfriend about it at the time. She's a doctor, and she helped me realize that what happened was because you were in pain, not because you wanted to hurt me." There's a hollow pang in my chest when I talk about her.

"Oh yeah, we get a few hours of internet time a week here; I saw you were dating again. That's wonderful, Jason. Are there wedding bells in the future?" She sounds genuinely happy for me, and I can't stop the few tears that begin to escape. I've never cried this much in my life.

"Well, actually. She just broke up with me. If I hadn't fucked it all up, we'd probably be living together right now."

"Oh Jason, I'm so sorry. But I can't imagine you messed up that badly. It's ok if you don't want to talk about it, but honestly, it would be nice to think about something other than my own mental health right now." She chuckles a bit self-consciously. And suddenly, I find myself desperate to share.

"I think I need to talk about it."

I end up spilling it all out. Every detail, well at least the important ones, my ex doesn't need to hear about our sex life. When I finish, the line is silent for a bit. I almost think she's hung up.

"Well, Jason. I won't lie; you did kind of mess up. But I think the party thing isn't the real issue here. Sure, she's mad, but as long as it works out with her job, she'll probably get over it fast. I mean, I don't know her, but it sounds like she's more hung up on the fact that you didn't stand up for yourself and your dreams. Maybe if you show her that you're stronger than you were that night, she'll forgive you?"

I see a tiny ray of hope for the first time in weeks. "You know what, Vanessa? I think you're right." A million ideas start popping into my head. I know exactly what I need to do to show her I love her and that I want to build a future that I'm proud of. But it's going to take some time, and fuck, that scares me. What if it takes too long?

"Thank you for listening. I'm so glad you called. Don't be a stranger, ok? I know we didn't end things on the best note, but I'm here if you need help."

"Ok," her voice is watery. I know she's probably crying. I can only imagine the emotional roller coaster phone calls like this are like. "I hope you win her back, Jason. Good luck."

We hang up, and my body is thrumming with energy. I look around my apartment, trying to find a piece of paper to write down all my ideas. But I can't find anything in the mess. Ok, I need to clean up first, then get cracking on winning my girl back.

There's no time to waste.

***

After spending nearly two straight weeks writing and getting my life back on track, I find myself shitting bricks in my car, trying to muster up the courage to enter my parents' home. Alexis was right. I need to be honest with them about my dreams. I have to push through my fear of rejection if I want any hope of repairing things with her.

My dashboard clock ticks to the top of the hour, and I've officially been sitting here in my car for over ten minutes. I have no doubt that my parents are inside wondering what the hell I'm waiting for. I take a few belly breaths to help calm my nervous system. While I'm not at the stage of going to therapy, I have forced myself to research some things. The internet is an enlightening place.

With my nerves at least calmed, I finally step out and enter their home.

"Darling! I'm so happy to see you," my mom attempts to nonchalantly come around the entry way corner to pull me into a hug, but I can tell she was probably hovering at the door until I started to make my way in. "Your father is in the living room; we have lunch all set up." When she moves to let go, I pull her closer, suddenly unable to stop our hug.

She hesitates only for a moment before her arms encircle me again and she squeezes just like she used to when I was young. It's the squeeze that does me in. Before I know it, tears are streaming down my face, and my whole body is shaking.

"Oh, dear lord, honey, what's wrong?" At the sound of my mother's distress, my father literally comes running from the other room. Skidding to a stop when he sees us. When we connect eyes, he immediately joins our hug, enveloping us both in his classic bear hug. The instant comfort I feel makes me cry even harder. To their credit, they don't ask anymore questions, they just hold me until I'm cried out, and can ask them to sit with me in the living room.

Once we're all seated, crammed together on the couch because neither wanted to be too far from me, I take a deep breath and say the words I've wanted to say to them for years.

"I'm quitting acting."

There's a pregnant pause, and I don't doubt that over my slumped shoulders my parents are exchanging a look in which they have an entire conversation with each other. I'm surprised when it's my father who speaks first.

"Way to freak us out. Your mom and I thought you were going to tell us something actually terrible. Like you were diagnosed with cancer." He relaxes back into the couch, as if all he felt was relief.

"You're not," I pause, trying to find the right words to describe my fears that won't hurt their feelings. "You're not mad that I won't be an actor like you two and Isla anymore?"

"No, of course not." My mom reaches to take my hand in hers, ducking her head down to catch my eyes. "Why would we ever be mad about something like that?" I can hear the hurt in her voice, which was exactly what I was trying to avoid. But I remind myself that the hurt isn't about me quitting the family vocation, it's about me thinking they'd have a negative reaction.

"I just. You guys always used to say 'we're an acting family' and I had this weird feeling that if I didn't become an actor just like you, that I'd be disappointing you. And the longer I waited to do anything about my fear, the harder it became to talk about.

And now I've risked my entire relationship with Alexis because of it." I take a big gulp of air and keep pushing. Because I need to get it all out.

"Growing up without you two home all the time was really hard. Harder than you realized. And I got in this habit, or belief maybe, that if I didn't do everything in my power to show you how amazing I was, that you wouldn't be proud of me. And once my career began, you both were just so excited and proud that I convinced myself you wouldn't support me if I chose to do something different with my life. And I know that's wrong, and just my imagination, but that anxiety I felt left no room for rational thought. But Alexis helped me realize I can't let my fears hold me back anymore. I need to live my life for me. Even if that means you're disappointed."

When I look over at my mom, she's quietly wiping tears from her eyes with her free hand. A quick glance at my dad confirms he's also crying. Apparently, we're a family of criers. If I wasn't close to tears again myself, I'd probably laugh.

My father sits up straight again and clasps my shoulder, turning me slightly so that we're looking at each other. "I could never not be proud of you. You could be a full-time barista and living in our home because you can't afford to live on your own and I'd still be proud of you. Because what you do for a living will *never* matter to your mother and I. The *only* thing we care about is if you're happy. Do you understand me?"

I nod, emotions clogging my throat. Deep, deep down, I knew this was how this conversation would go. But actually experiencing it in reality has created a firestorm of conflicting feelings.

"The only thing I could possibly be upset about is if you let any of this steal away your chance to get Alexis back. I want her as my daughter-in-law, and I want some grandbabies soon. So, how can we help you win her back?"

I should have known my mother would find a way to make this about grandchildren.

"Well, I have some ideas. But I'm not sure it's going to be enough." It really shouldn't surprise me, but I find myself filled with awe as my parents go into full strategy mode to help me win her back. Fuck, I hope she forgives me.

Chapter 37

Alexis

It's been three months since I ended things with Jason, and I still feel just as hollow as I did then. I started as an attending officially last week, and even that couldn't fill this hole inside me.

I spend every free moment at the hospital, picking up shifts when allowed and taking every available on-call possible. I'm pretty sure Slinky thinks I'm dead each time I'm gone for more than a day, because she goes crazy when I come home. She's pretty much the only thing holding me together at this point.

Nique, Allison, and Tristan have all tried to help. But even girls' nights and doing things like facials or shopping just leave me feeling worse rather than better. They try to be understanding and helpful, but they don't exactly get why I ended things. Maybe it's because they're all romantics, but on more than one occasion, they've tried to convince me to try to reconcile.

But every time I let myself think, *maybe*, my dad's voice rings in my head. *I almost lost sight of my career. I just don't want you to make the same mistakes I did.* What if I let him back into my life and nothing changes, and I suddenly find myself in an unhappy relationship with my career on the line? Maybe if there was a sign that Jason was trying to work on his insecurities I would feel differently, but after three months of radio silence, I'm starting to lose any hope that we might be able to work through this.

I stare down our hallway toward his unit every time I come home. And I think, *what if I just go down and knock*? But my feet never move.

I'm just numb.

But the worst question of all keeps me awake despite how exhausted I am. *What if I made a mistake?*

***

It's nearing midday, and I'm just getting back after my lunch break. I'm parked at the nurse's station, about to pull out a tablet to see who's next when dispatch calls. From the way the nurse sits up straighter, I know this call is for a serious incoming patient. Probably another car accident. It feels like there's been a lot of those lately.

She gets off the call and immediately turns to me. "We've got a mass casualty event. Multiple patients with gunshot wounds, there was a shooter at a movie set."

My heart nearly stops. But no, this is L.A. I'm sure it's not his movie. But even though I know the odds are low, I can't stop myself from asking, "Did they say which movie?"

The nurse doesn't look up; she's too busy starting to call in doctors and other staff. We're going to need all hands on deck for this. "I think they said something like *Primordial Fallout*?"

"Do you mean *Primogenesis Fallout*?"

"Oh yeah, that's the one. Two buses are incoming with the first victims. I've already paged Dr. Jordan."

I barely hear her; my mind is reeling.

This can't be happening. Don't let him be hurt, don't let him be hurt.

Dr. Jordan meets me in the ambulance bay, gowned up and ready to help me do the same. I'm a robot, throwing on gear from memory, not because I'm paying attention. She gives me a weird look but doesn't comment. I'm not sure I would even hear her over the ringing in my ears.

The first ambulance squeals in, the doors opening before it even comes to a complete stop.

"We've got a thirty-year-old male, two gunshot wounds to the chest, one to the leg." Dr. Jordan steps up, and her team takes over. I try to see the patient's face and catch a glimpse. The man's hair is dark, so not Jason. It only eases my worry slightly.

The driver comes out and rounds the truck, beginning to reset before they drive out again.

"Do you know how many patients we're getting?"

"No, Doctor, just that as soon as my partner gets back, we need to go back to the scene."

I nod, trying to calm my nerves. This will be one of the most important days in my career so far; I need to get my head in the game.

"Do you," I hesitate, not knowing if I should even ask. But if I don't, it will make me worry. "Do you know if Jason Adams was on set or was injured?"

The guy gives me a weird look, probably wondering why the hell I'm asking. "No doctor, I'm sorry, I don't know."

Before I can press for more information, the next ambulance pulls in. My team comes up behind me, ready for the patient transfer.

"We've got a twenty-four-year-old female, one wound in the arm and a graze across her temple." As I listen to their report, I let the medical professional inside me take over. This woman needs me, and I won't let her down. I'll have to worry about Jason later.

***

My shift ended hours ago, but I haven't left. I treated six patients and lost two. But I still haven't learned if Jason was on set. I've called him maybe a hundred times, straight to voicemail. Texts remain unanswered. Jason is many things, but he isn't petty. He would never ignore me like this just to spite me. And I *know* it's the movie that he was considering. I'll never forgive myself if he was there.

I'm doing another pass of the ICU, checking charts, trying to figure out who is who. I interrogate every person who isn't injured that I pass. But no one seems to know. But if he isn't here... oh god, I don't even want to consider it.

I feel myself starting to unravel. My breath is coming in quick, and it feels like the walls are closing in. The doctor in me is noting that I'm having a panic attack. But I can't stop it.

I barely make it to an on-call room before I fall apart. I'm on the floor, rocking myself, trying to self-soothe while sobbing. I can't let our last conversation be the last thing I ever say to him. He can't be gone. He can't. All of a sudden, everything I was mad about seem dumb. Who cares if he wasn't ready to stick up for himself to Steven? What does it matter that being at that party put a ding in my career? Why did I just shut down instead of helping him? *None* of that matters if he's dead.

What he took the role because I walked away? What have I done?

I'm not exactly sure how long I'm in there, sitting in the dark. But eventually, I feel someone open the door quietly. A warm arm comes around my shoulders and pulls me close. When I look up, it's Tristan. How did she find me?

"There've been complaints of a doctor crying her eyes out in this hall." Must have said that out loud, I guess. "After I saw the news, I had a feeling it was you. Then I asked some of the ICU nurses, and they said you've been frantically checking charts to see if Jason was brought in."

Just hearing his name brings fresh tears to my eyes. Please, please, please let him be alright.

"Honey, he's ok. Or at least, ok enough to not be here or on the news. They've announced all the victims who died, and Jason isn't on the list. He's not hurt."

"Oh, thank fuck." I fall into Tristan's chest, sobbing anew. The relief is almost painful. I don't know what I would have done had he been there. She rubs my back, cooing softly, instructing me to breathe in... and breathe out. It takes a while, but I'm finally able to calm down.

"I was so scared Tristan. I thought I had lost him, our future. What if – What if he had been there? What if he had *died* and we lost the chance to get married. Have kids? I want to have his kids Tristan!"

She chuckles, knowing kids has never really been on my radar historically. But with Jason, I can see them so clearly. Cute, rosy cheeked, blond haired green-eyed mini humans. I love them and they don't even exist yet.

"Thank you. For looking and finding me. I think I need to go home."

"Do you want me to call a ride?"

"No, I'm ok. I just need to see him."

Tristan nods, helping me to stand before going back to her workday. She happens to be on nights this week.

The whole way home, I try to rehearse what I'm going to say. How do I apologize and get him to forgive me?

I'm not sure why I even tried to prepare, because I'm crying the moment I'm in front of his door. I knock once, just barely cognizant that it's very late. But after a few seconds of no response, I knock again. And again. And again, until I'm pounding for what feels like forever, but is probably only a few minutes at most. To be fair, it is almost three in the morning.

And when I see him? Hair rumpled, eyes squinting at the light and an adorable crease in his cheek from his pillow, I collapse.

He catches me.

CHAPTER 38

JASON

"What? Alexis?" It takes half a second for my exhausted brain to realize that she's sobbing in my arms. I caught her on instinct, and I'm now very confused.

"Baby, what is it? What's wrong? Are you hurt?" She doesn't answer, just starts crying harder. I'm starting to panic. What if she was attacked? She shakes her head, pulling me tight against her, holding on as if her life depends on it.

Not wanting this to continue in the hall, I pull her inside and shut the door. Once we have privacy, I wrap my arms around her tight and just hold her. I have no idea why she's here, but I'm not going to pass up the opportunity to hold her. To breathe her in. Fuck, I missed her.

Eventually, she calms down enough to talk. Her eyes are bloodshot, cheeks chapped, and I wish I could take it all away, whatever it is.

"There was a shooting." She hiccups, fresh tears falling down her face. I do my best to wipe them away. "It was on the set of

Primogenesis Fallout. And, I thought... fuck, I thought you had signed on and were there, and I kept asking people who were on the scene if you were there, but no one knew. And I kept checking the ICU patients over and over again, but you weren't there. And I thought that the worst had happened, that you had died and that we never got the chance to repair things and be together, and I fell apart. Then Tristan found me and told me you were ok." A new wave of tears spill over her red cheeks , and she can't keep going.

"It's ok, baby, I understand. I heard about it on the news but didn't know what set it was on. I would have texted – shit, my phone's still on Do Not Disturb isn't it?" She just nods, unable to talk. I feel awful, I needed to concentrate, so I turned it on, it never occurred to me that she'd think I was there. But of course, why wouldn't she? The last she knew, I was giving in and letting Steven bully me into signing on.

I kiss the top of her head, rubbing her back as she cries. Fuck, if our roles were reversed? I don't know what I would do.

Eventually, she's able to calm down again, and I can tell she's exhausted. Right now the only thing that will help is sleep.

"Come on, Sweet Cheeks, let's get you home and into bed."

She doesn't argue as I bundle her up and walk us down to her apartment. Once I get her inside, I immediately take her to the bathroom and help her wash her face and put PJs on. As soon as she's in bed, Slinky immediately comes in and lies on her chest, purring quietly.

"Try to get some sleep, ok? I'll talk to you tomorrow." I try to leave, but she grabs my arm.

"Wait! Where are you going? Don't leave," her voice cracks, and I can already see new tears forming, "please." She whispers.

"Home, back to bed?" I'm confused. Despite all that's happened tonight, we haven't talked anything through, I wouldn't dream of assuming I'd stay the night. And I'm not sure I should.

"But, I thought, I thought you would stay..." she pauses, her face twisting in pain, "I'm too late, aren't I? You've moved on."

Let me tell you, I was way too happy over her thinking she was too late. Not because she looked devastated, but because it means I have a chance to win her back.

I kneel, taking her hand, and brushing back her hair. "No, you haven't lost me. I've been working really hard to be the man I want to be. Not just for you, but for me too. I don't want to just rush right back in, without us talking it out. Right now, your emotions are shot. You need rest and to come down from the emotional day. Then we can talk it out. I'll stay until you fall asleep, then I'm returning to my apartment to finish what I'm working on. Ok?"

"This is stupid."

"I know it is, sweetheart, but it's what I need to do to feel like I'm worthy of your love. Do you understand?"

The fact that she came to me first makes my heart soar, it gives me hope that things will work out for us. But despite that, I'm not quite ready. As stupid as it sounds, I want to finish what I started first.

She frowns, but nods. "I don't, but I'll allow it. Just don't take too long."

I lean forward and kiss her brow.

"I won't, I promise." I climb in next to her and let her snuggle in close, wrapping my arms securely around her. It doesn't take long for her body to relax and her breathing to even. It's pure torture, but I know I'll regret it if I don't finish what I've started.

When I go to bed, I feel hope, real hope. I'm getting my girl back.

CHAPTER 39

ALEXIS

TWO DAYS.

That motherfucker makes me wait two entire days before he starts his 'plan.'

He did text me multiple times, but it's not the same.

And a "patience is a virtue" text isn't really something that would inspire more patience. The exact opposite, really.

So, when I get home from my shift two days later and see a package in front of my door with a note, I shriek in joy and do a happy dance. I honestly don't care what he has planned; I just need him to come home.

I haul the gift inside and shut my door, ripping off the note like I'm She-Hulk or something.

Alexis,

The night we met, all I could think was, 'who is this crazy beautiful woman wearing a unicorn onesie and chasing her maniac cat? I like her.' I never thought we would build the relationship we did or that I would find myself missing Slinky almost as much as I've missed you.

I hope you like what's in the box. I have one too, so we can match during movie marathons.

I love you so much; it hurts sometimes.

Jason

P.S. Please tell Slinky I have a monthly order of her treats set up; she deserves a lifetime supply for being the reason we met.

I don't even know what's in the box, but I'm already sobbing. I know I'll love it. When I finally get it out, I cry even harder. He had onesies made with Slinky's face printed all over it. It's dorky and obnoxious, but it's perfect.

Underneath the onesie is a thick envelope. I pull it out, a little startled by how heavy it is. When I pull out the contents, it's another spiral-bound book, with a note taped to the front.

Alexis, light of my life,

You were right that night. I did give in to my insecurities and fears. I didn't stand up for myself, and it nearly cost me the only thing that truly mattered. You.

I've spent every day since building myself back into the man I want to be so that when I look at you, I'll know I'm worthy. I told Steven I'm not taking on a new project for the foreseeable future. He's not happy, but I think he understands I'm not kidding around. I even told my parents. Everything. I thought they'd try to talk me out of it or be disappointed. But you were right. They love me and thought I loved acting as much as they did. They're probably waiting by the phone right now, hoping to get the call that you've taken me back. They love you already. How could they not?

In this envelope is what I've been working on. I wrote a script. A movie script, and I'm going to try to get it made. It was hard at first. I was so depressed after you ended things; I wasn't sure I could write at all. But once I started, I suddenly couldn't stop. I'm forcing Steven to help me shop it with some production companies. Who knows, maybe this is the start of something new?

I want you to read it first, then come see me, even if it's at three in the morning again. I hope you like it.

I love you so much.

Jason

P.S. I love you; I love you; I love you.

I haven't even started reading, and I'm already crying. I almost want to skip reading and go straight to him. But I know he desperately needs me to do this his way, so I quickly put on the onesie (because, how could I not, I'm about to basically read a movie), settle on the couch, and begin reading.

He wrote our story. It's a little different; the main male character is a rockstar, the female lead is a veterinarian, and Slinky is weirdly a ferret? But the bones of our story are there. And fuck, it's funny. And sweet. And a little sexy. And by the end, I'm crying so hard I can barely see the script. The second I read the words 'the end', I'm *running* out of my apartment. I glance at my smartwatch and laugh; it's nearly three A.M.

When I reach his door, I don't bother knocking; I just know he left it unlocked for me. And then there he is, sitting on his couch, also wearing the Slinky onesie like the complete dork he is, head in his hands, knee jiggling.

Then he hears me. His head pops up. His eyes are so full of hope and love that I can't help my smile.

"Before we do anything, I need to say something." He looks green, clearly nervous about what I have to say. He nods, swallowing visibly.

"You, Jason Adams, were never unworthy. You have always been and will always be the love of my life, and I am so sorry that I let my fear make me think otherwise. I love my gifts, but I don't need them. I only need you. Understood?" He nods again; I can see moisture in his eyes. He needed me to say that, even if he didn't realize it.

"Now, get your ass over here, Hollywood. I need to kiss my man." A huge grin splits across his face as he comes bolting across the room and sweeps me into his arms. Our mouths crash together, quickly sealing while our hands scrabble to unzip the suddenly inconvenient onesies and touch. How could I ever believe I could live without him?

Finally, our onesies are off, and we both gasp as our naked bodies meet. It never ceases to amaze me how connected we feel, even after weeks of being apart.

"I'm going to make love to you and then fuck you until you can't see straight. Does that work for you, Doc?"

"Yes, yes, yes." I moan as his lips find his favorite spot on my neck. The feeling of him sucking hard and most definitely giving me a hickey sends a thrill down my spine. I need him *now*.

"Jason?"

"Hmmm?"

"Bed. Now."

"Yes, doctor." We both laugh as he throws me over his shoulder and takes off down the hall. He pretends to yelp when I take a bite out of his juicy ass. He loves it when I do that.

Instead of tossing me on the bed and going all Dom on me, he sets me down gently. Spreading me across the bed. He doesn't join me immediately, just steps back and takes me in.

"Fuck, you're the most beautiful person in the world. Did I tell you yet how much I love you?"

I shake my head, trying to look upset. "No. I think you need to tell me again and again. Preferably, followed by a few orgasms?" He chuckles and finally joins me. Leaning down to give me a sweet kiss on my lips.

He then continues down my body, taking his time kissing and nipping at every sensitive spot. He spends several minutes on each breast, teasing my nipples with his teeth before taking me into his mouth and sucking. By the time he moves on, I'm nearly incoherent, the pulse between my legs throbbing so hard, I'm surprised I haven't come yet.

Then finally, finally, his head is between my thighs. He takes a moment, clearly soaking it all in, before his mouth lands on my clit and his fingers seek out my G-spot. I'm so wet already that his fingers don't even have to work to get in. My back arches off the bed as he gently sucks.

"Yes, yes, yes! Don't stop, Jason; I'm almost there!" My fingers are diving through his hair, twisting the strands with my fingers. I can feel him smile against me.

He's slow at first, then starts to pick up the pace until I'm thrashing on the bed, begging him to let me come. But instead of doing what he knows will get me off, he stops.

"What are you doing?"

He kisses his way back up my body until our faces are level. "When I make you come for the first time in months, it's going to be on my cock."

His lips crash into mine again, and I can taste my own arousal. My hips roll against his, trying to find the right angle for him to finally get inside me. With my legs wrapped around his waist, after what feels like forever, he finally lines up and slams home.

We both have to stop kissing in order to moan in pleasure. Fuck, does it feel somehow better than before? He fills me up so good, and I know I feel tight and hot for him. It doesn't escape my notice that we didn't use a condom, and as if he reads my thoughts, he says.

"No more condoms, no more separation. I'm ready to spend my life with you and make babies. So, when you're ready, we'll take out your IUD and get to work."

"Me too Jason, me too. All I could think about when I thought you were dead is how I'd lost the chance to have a life with you, have kids. That nearly broke me. I don't want to waste another minute of our life together." My heart is so full, it might burst.

Soon he has me panting again, not thinking about babies or the future. Just this moment right now. With him inside me, making each other feel good.

He reaches down and starts rubbing my clit *just* right. And I'm off, orgasm rolling through so violently that I scream his name. A moment later, he's falling with me, and I feel him pump inside me. His forehead connects with mine, and I can see all the love I'll ever need reflected back at me.

"I love you."

"And I love you."

EPILOGUE

Five years later

Alexis

I am positively giddy right now as I walk through the front
entrance of our house, Slinky doing her best to trip me as I
remove my shoes. Even in her old age, she wants constant attention. We bought this sweet little bungalow three years ago after
my parents officially announced they were done traveling and
ready to settle into retirement. These last few years haven't been
easy. But they've been full of love and laughter, and I couldn't
be happier.

Jason's writing career didn't go exactly as we thought. The
first script he wrote was optioned and made into a movie. It
was a hit, but he couldn't find traction when he tried again.
Not a lot of companies want to take a chance on romcoms if
they don't prove themselves in the reading market first. So, at
my gentle prodding, he turned the script into a novel. And let
me tell ya, the romance reading community *loves* him. I mean,

who wouldn't? After writing two more books, he decided to try a different genre and is currently working on his first Sci-Fi. I can't wait to read it.

My career has progressed beautifully. I'm still at the same hospital in the ER, and I think I'm about to be offered Dr. Jordan's job. She let it slip last month that she's retiring and put me up for the promotion. Jason thinks I have it in the bag. I'm keeping my fingers crossed.

I also record a podcast on weekends with a group of other women doctors from various fields. We were first brought together for a panel at a conference and were a hit. And within a month, we'd joined forces to make the podcast. We primarily focus on answering the public's questions about their health concerns, but also discuss current events in the medical field and how public policy affects medicine. At this point, I'm now more likely to get recognized on the street than my dear husband. Something I never expected, but Jason thinks it's hilarious.

A year into our marriage, we decided we were ready to try getting pregnant. I was getting nervous since my mom struggled so much and worried I would too. And as it turns out, I wasn't wrong. After two miscarriages, and dozens of negative tests, Jason already wanted to stop trying. He was so ready to be a father, and each disappointment weighed heavily on him. We decided to take a break from actively trying, no more charts or thermometers, and if after a year, we still weren't pregnant, we'd look into IVF. That was six months ago, and I'm currently five months pregnant.

He has no idea.

Honestly, I'm starting to show a bit and have been feeling crummy for months. The man is an idiot sometimes. But he's my idiot.

When I step out into our backyard, he's on a picnic blanket with Charlotte and Zachary, our niblings. They're three now, and we love having them over for visits.

"Auntie *Yexi*! Auntie *Yexi!* You're back!" They pop up and charge for my legs, nearly taking me out. I love they still can't say their L's yet. It will be a sad day when I become Auntie Lexi instead of Auntie Yexi. Maybe they'll never grow out of it?

"Hey, you little monsters, let your aunt sit down. Don't knock her over." I smile down at my gorgeous husband. Even after four years, it's still a shock to say I'm married to Jason Adams. He has gained a little gray at his temples this year, and I'm obsessed. As I settle onto the blanket, I buss him a kiss on the cheek. Before he can take it further, I pull back and bring out the bag I brought out.

"Charlotte, Zach, I have a little present for you both."

"Presents? YES!" Both jump up and down, aggressively yelling and punching the air. Three-year-old's, man, they're something else.

"Alright, please sit down while I give you your gift, and make sure to hold yours up high so Uncle Jay can see them." They nod, immediately plopping onto the blanket. I hand them their matching tie-dye shirts, biting my lip as they unfold and hold them up. Zach's is upside down, but you can still read what's printed there.

#1 COUSIN

I glance over at Jason, and he looks confused. Oh, my sweet husband, sometimes he's clueless. So, I pull out another shirt and hand it to him.

"Here, I got you one too." I'm barely keeping a huge smile off my face as he opens it up and stares at it. Like the twins', it says *#1 DAD*.

After a beat, I realize he's still staring. So, I pull out my last clue. I sit up and unzip my hoodie, revealing my matching shirt that says, you guessed it: *#1 MOM*.

He stares at my shirt, then at my face, then back at his shirt, then back at my face. I can't stop the tears that are starting to spill over.

"Does this?" He chokes up, tears filling his eyes. "Does this mean you're pregnant?"

"Yes, baby, I am. And I waited a long, long time to tell you. I just had a doctor's appointment, I'm five months along, and the baby is doing great. She's confident we'll have a healthy baby in a few months." I smile and put my hand on my softly swelling stomach.

"We're going to be parents!" He laughs, pulling me against his body, lips in my hair, hand instantly covering mine. "Babe, we're going to be parents!"

"I know!" We're both smiling at each other, hands on my belly, completely ignoring the two toddlers now running around screaming that they're going to be cousins. Nothing could make this day more perfect.

***

Four months later

Jason

I'm doing everything I can to not cry right now. I'm in a hospital lounger, my sweet baby girl on my chest, doing some skin-to-skin time with papa while Alexis dozes next to us in the bed. We're both exhausted after twenty-five hours of labor, but now we have our sweet girl, and it was all worth it.

Fuck, it was so hard seeing Alexis in so much pain. I hate that I could barely do anything for her. At one point, I think I told her we were done with one baby; I won't do that to her again. And she fucking laughed and said, "Yeah, we'll see about that." Is she crazy?

But when I look at this little human we created, I think maybe she's right. I'm not sure how I could love her any more than I did when she was just a peanut in the womb, but now that she's here, I feel like my heart is about to explode out of my chest.

"When we get home," I tell her quietly, hoping I don't wake Alexis. "Your best friend, Slinky, will be so happy to meet you. She's been keeping your bassinet nice and warm for you." I gently run a finger down her downy cheek, finding it hard to swallow. This love is overwhelming.

Our little girl begins to stir, making sweet baby noises and nuzzling. Her eyes are still closed, but her mouth is pursed; I think she might be ready to try the boob again. I read somewhere that fathers can use their own nipples to soothe their babies if mom isn't around, and even though I know it would be completely natural, I can't quite make myself do it. She begins to squawk, and I quickly stand up, cradling her while gently waking Alexis. As much as I wish I could let her just sleep, we need to try again to feed her.

"Is she looking for the boob?" Her voice is rough and groggy, but she's already reaching for our baby. First, I have her sit forward, so I can scoot in behind her, careful not to jostle her too much. Once Alexis' back is settled comfortably against my chest, I help her undo the hooks of her maternity dress.

We tried nursing a few hours ago but struggled. Baby didn't quite latch, and it was painful for Alexis. Nobody truly prepares you for how helpless you'll feel when your baby doesn't feed right away. Newborns can go way longer than you would expect, designed to handle not nursing if things aren't perfect. But every new parent thinks it won't be them until it is. It's terrifying.

But this time, after a few misses, the baby latches comfortably and begins nursing with abandon. Her tiny little fist opening and closing softly against Alexis' chest.

We both stare down at her in awe; she's so perfect. I kiss Alexis' hairline, smoothing back the strands. She sighs, relaxing into me even more.

"We really need to name her."

I laugh. We've been saying that for hours now. Every name option we had prepared over these last few months just wasn't right. And now we're scrambling. "I know. How about I'll just start listing names, and you just tell me when we get to one you like?"

"Hmmm, seems like a faulty system, but sure."

"Margaret."

"No, too close to Martha. And don't you dare suggest anything close to my mom's name. Not happening."

Ok.

"Esther."

"No. Come on, she's not ninety."

"Ava?"

"No."

"Lauren?"

"No."

"Selene?"

"No."

Rebecca?"

"No."

"Brexley."

"What are we, granola people?"

"Man, you're tough. Let me think." I pretend to mull it over when in reality, I've had the perfect name saved for months.

"Ok, I have one. What about Willa?"

She pauses, running a finger across our baby's perfect little brow.

"Is that it, sweet girl? Is your name Willa?" Our baby slowly blinks her eyes open, seemingly looking right at us as if to say *yeah, that's me.*

"Willa, it is then." I kiss Alexis on the cheek again, then sweep my hand over Willa's baby head, readjusting her tiny newborn hat. She's so soft and warm; I want to cry every time I look at her.

"What about her last name? We never really talked about it." Honestly, I haven't really thought about it myself. I've been so focused on just making sure Alexis and Willa were healthy that it didn't cross my mind that we should probably decide on a last name. When we got married, neither of us changed our names. Alexis had all her doctor licensure under Masters, and I had been building a name for myself in the romance genre. Neither of us wanted to go through the hassle of changing things. So we didn't. But now we have a kid.

"I kind of hate our names hyphenated. Adams-Masters or Masters-Adams. They just sound weird. And long." I nod. I completely agree. Then it hits me. The perfect solution.

"What if we make her middle name Adams and her last name Masters?"

Alexis turns, careful not to jostle the nursing baby but still trying to see my face. "Are you serious? It won't bother you to not have the same last name?"

"Nah, we'll still share a name, even if it's her middle one. Plus, if she grows up and wants to, she can always change it." Honestly, all I care about right now is that both my girls are healthy.

"Ok, but if you change your mind..."

"I won't."

We sit there for a bit, watching our baby.

"I love you."

"And I love you."

We sit together in silence, watching Willa nurse, cocooned in a bubble of love and safety. Eventually, Alexis and Willa drift off to sleep, and I just keep holding them, feeling like the luckiest man in the world.

ACKNOWLEDGMENTS

Writing a book takes a village. No book exists simply because the author thought it into existence (that would be nice though). So, there's a whole list of people I'd like to thank for helping me on my journey to publish my first book!

First, to my cats, Runt, Pickles, and the late great Chicken Nugget. You guys kept me entertained and sustained while I wrote, and edited, and edited again. I'm not sure I would have gotten through this without your steadfast kitty love.

Next, is of course, my family and friends, who have always been supportive of my writing and bookworm tendencies. Without you all, I definitely would not have been able to pull this off. Special shout-out to Savannah for being the first reader of the first draft.

I can't forget to thank my editor Jenn Herrington, Fresh Look Editorial! I've never had a professional review my work before, so it was pretty scary. You made sure I felt comfortable with the process, while still pushing me to hone my skills. This book would not be where it is today without you! Thank you!

Another special shout-out is required for Charis (@charisjb.studio on I.G.) for the amazing cover art and design! You somehow managed the take exactly what was in my head and translate it into the perfect cover! I can't thank you enough!

Giant thank you to my ARC Readers! Your enthusiasm and willingness to read a book from an author you've never heard of literally brought tears to my eyes. I am so thankful you took a chance on my book.

And last, I need to thank past me for being brave enough to do this. Writing is deeply personal and it's incredibly daunting thinking about it being out in the world. Little 10 year old me, who could barely read, would never have guessed I'd become an avid reader, let alone an author. I still can't quite believe I'm actually doing this.

Actually, the last person I need to thank is you, dear reader, for picking up and reading this book. I hope you enjoyed reading, just as much as I enjoyed writing, *Cat's Outta the Bag*. And I hope there'll be many more in the future.